Pictures, 1918

Pictures, 1918

JEANETTE INGOLD

Harcourt Brace & Company

San Diego   New York   London

Library of Congress Cataloging-in-Publication Data
Ingold, Jeanette.
Pictures, 1918/Jeanette Ingold.
p.   cm.
Summary: Coming of age in a rural Texas community in 1918,
fifteen-year-old Asia assists in the local war effort, contemplates
romance with a local boy, and expands her horizons through
her pursuit of photography.
ISBN 0-15-201809-3
[1. Photography—Fiction.   2. Country life—Texas—Fiction.
3. Texas—Fiction.   4. World War, 1914–1918—
United States—Fiction.]   I. Title.
PZ7.I533Pi   1998
[Fic]—dc21   98-5229

Text set in Simoncini Garamond
Designed by Lydia D'moch
First edition
A C E F D B
Printed in the United States of America

For my grandmothers,
Bonnie Cain Reilly Bergeron
and
Julia Coila Norman Henry

1

THE EVENING OF THE FIRE we've been playing cards on the screened side porch—Homer and Grandmama and me. When we finish, Grandmama says, "I believe I'll walk out to the privy," and my brother runs off, calling, "You put stuff away, Asia."

So I gather the cards and carry our iced tea glasses to the kitchen before heading out back myself.

The dry Texas air is just at that line it reaches some early March evenings, hot day on one side and night chill on the other. Above, a faint band of stars looks to stretch clear across heaven. And from inside the house come the sounds of my sister, May, trying to learn guitar. She finally finds a few notes that go together, and the plucked chords twang into the night.

A dark shape moves beyond the chicken house, framed by the thick limbs of our pecan tree.

"That you, Grandmama?" I call. She shouldn't be off the path, not in the dark, not with her brittle bones. No, that can't be her....

A light flickers in one high-up, barred window of the coop and then disappears. *Who would be gathering eggs at this hour?* I go over to see.

"Mama?" I say, opening the door.

Inside, the smell of kerosene engulfs me, stronger than the sweet, hot smell of the dozen frightened chickens huddled in one corner, huddled and flapping and squawking. They are as far as they can get from a low fire that licks over straw on the packed-earth floor and climbs twine that hangs from a high-up hook.

I rush in, trying to get to the chickens, beating at the flames. "Papa! Mama!" I yell. "Fire! Fire! FIRE!"

Even as I'm yelling the flames shoot higher, flaring and jumping until every nest box blazes.

I fight the flames as long as I can stand to, beating them with a feed sack and my shoes. Then suddenly they join into a rushing orange wall that pushes me out the door.

People are running my way now, and I can hear neighbors' voices shouting on the street, doors banging, and men calling out orders. Someone yells to ring the fire department, and someone else calls that the fire truck is on its way.

Then the running figures form into rough lines and begin passing along buckets from the cistern, passing them along to Papa, because it's his chicken house. Nick Grissom tears past me with another boy; the two of them run with buckets as though they are racing each other to put out the fire.

For long moments I watch people fling whorls of water on flames that grow and grow, even as the fire truck's clanging bell draws closer.

"It's going," someone says, and the words release me.

I run then as fast as I can around to the far side of the chicken house to the lean-to that my family calls Asia's Zoo.

It's where I keep my pets at night. Old One-Eye, my tortoise. Zoey and her latest batch of kittens, already all spoken for. The jackrabbit baby that I'm raising on a bottle. His name is Straw Bit, and he stretches up tall against his cage whenever he sees me so I'll take him out and feed him.

When I open the door, Zoey flings herself through it; then turns and races back to her kittens. She grabs one by its neck skin and disappears into the dark with it.

I snatch up the basket with the others and run to the shelter of the house.

Then, rushing back, I pick up One-Eye, his feet scratching and flailing and his head thrusting from his shell. It takes both my hands to carry him. Again I run to safety.

And in that time, the flames stream around the corner of the chicken house and jump across the lean-to door, spread inside to straw, and light up boxes and food bins and Straw Bit's cage.

"No!" I scream, and my scream rips through the night, going on and on as I run that endless distance back to the lean-to. "Noooooooooo..."

And then someone, one of the men, is holding me, gripping my arms with fingers that won't pry loose. "Stop, Asia," he says, "you can't go in there."

"Nooooo..."

Beyond the flames Straw Bit bounds up against the top of his cage, springs on his hind legs and falls and springs and falls. Springs until the flames get so high I can't see him anymore.

After that the hands let go. For a few moments I stand alone feeling the sideways glances of neighbors, even of strangers drawn by the fire. May, helping Mama wet down the garden shed, calls, "Asia...;" and I know she wants to come to me.

Then my grandmother steps between me and the others, wrapping thin arms around me and pulling me to her.

"Oh, Grandmama," I whisper. My insides are so tight with hurt they keep tears from coming. "Oh, Grandmama."

"There, child," she says. "There, there. I'm sorry."

I WISH I HAD two pictures, photographs that nobody has taken.

The first one I want is of the dark shape that I glimpsed, a picture that I could look at until I knew who put kerosene in the chicken house and left it to burn.

The other I long for is a real picture of my jackrabbit baby. I want it to wipe out from my mind how he looked leaping behind flames.

And, also, I need that second photograph to fill in

what I can't remember, to tell me if he had dark patches on all four feet or just three.

My memory is all that is left of Straw Bit, and anyone, even an animal, deserves to leave more on earth than a memory.

2

BY MORNING THE CHICKEN HOUSE and lean-to aren't anything but blowing soot and smell, charred timber, and a few strands of twisted wire.

I cradle one of Zoey's kittens in my arms, keeping my eyes turned away from the ruins of the fire but unable to shut my nose to the sour, acrid smell. All the spring wind of West Texas isn't enough to blow the air fresh.

The end of a fire—it reminds me of a motion picture May and I went to, one that showed a Belgian battlefield where there wasn't anything left but a burned-up house. Is this what the war does to whole countries? Makes them look and smell like this?

Zoey, who has always before trusted me with her kittens, nudges and worries until I return her baby to her. She pushes it against the others to make a furry ball of family she can wrap herself around.

I reach down for a piece of singed hair that is hanging loose from her tail. Under the black, breaking ends, the fur is silver-gray threaded through with orange. I run a finger over its softness before slipping the tuft into my skirt pocket to keep.

Papa calls me over to where he's standing with a couple of friends at the edge of the rubble. They've been talking, probing the mess with their boots. "I can't understand it," my father is saying. "It must have been deliberately set. But why?"

He turns my way. "Asia, tell me again about what you saw."

As I've been doing all morning, I think of that dark shape I'd first taken for Grandmama.

"I didn't see much." My words are hesitant because the harder I think, the more uncertain I am of the memory. "I called out, but no one answered."

"But it was a person, Asia?"

"I think so. I'm not sure. It could have been just a shadow...and then there was the chicken house to go to, and the..." My voice falters when I try to say *fire,* the wobbly word overridden by Mama calling, "Chester, Chester!"

She's hurrying from the house, carrying the small kerosene can that we keep for filling lamps when the electricity goes out.

"Chester, look," she says, showing him how it swings easily in her hand. "This is empty, and I know it was almost full yesterday. I checked, thinking that with all this wind..."

Papa flushes angrily, and I can see why. Someone setting fire to *our* things, with *our* kerosene.

Mama frowns. "...and whoever, he put the can back

where it belonged when he was done. It doesn't make sense."

Grandmama, who has followed her out, nods in agreement. "It doesn't," she says.

"Asia," Papa asks, "can't you remember anything more? Anything?"

All I can do is shake my head. I didn't look long enough at that dark shape, or close enough.

Suddenly Nick Grissom is at my side, though I didn't hear him come up. I'm glad to slip off with him and get away from all those frustrated eyes demanding that I tell them what I don't know.

"Asia," he says, "I'm really sorry." His neck and ears redden the way they always do when he's feeling strongly about something. "I was so busy trying to help put out the fire, I didn't remember your animals in time."

I can hear his misery for me. Nick is a neighbor and my longest, best friend, though he's a year older and a class ahead, a senior.

"I didn't think fast enough, either," I tell him. "Besides, I saw how hard you were throwing water . . . you and that guy with you. Who was that?"

"Boy Blackwell. He's my cousin from Louisiana."

"Is he visiting with his family?"

"Just him."

Nick scoops up one of Zoey's kittens to pet, and Zoey lets him do it with less fuss than she gave me.

"But what I came for, Asia," Nick says, "is to tell you I'll stop by the lumberyard this afternoon and get some scrap boards to make a pen for One-Eye. He'll need it."

I nod. The old tortoise won't survive long without protection from foxes and coyotes.

And then Grandmama joins us. "Hello, Nick," she says.

She hands me a letter—"Asia, honey, will you please post this?"—and two dimes: "And then you and Nick go on to Mr. Peat's and have yourselves ice-cream sodas. You need cheering."

My grandmama. I know what she's up to. Matchmaking between Nick and me. Despite how sad I am, I have to smile. I doubt Nick will ever think of me in any way but as his best friend, and I've told Grandmama that more than once, but she never listens. Now she gives me a little push. "Go on, you two," she says. "A soda will do you good."

I roll my eyes to let Grandmama know she isn't putting anything over on me. And that I love her for trying.

Then, from nowhere and without warning, a dreadful feeling rushes through me. Not a feeling I could put words to, but a vague thought that I had Straw Bit and now I don't, and maybe it can be like that with people, too.

Then the feeling is gone and I'm saying, "Come on, Nick, before Homer sees us and asks himself along."

We move fast, but even so, when we turn the corner onto Mockingbird Street I see my little brother already by the front gate, Grandmama's hand firmly on his shoulder.

———

LATER, AFTER FINISHING work down at his father's newspaper, Nick returns. He brings with him an armload of lumber and chicken wire, a Schroeder Lumber Company tag hanging from the wire.

"Nick, did you buy all this?" I ask. "I'll pay you back."

"No need," he says. "It's mostly scraps, and Mr. Schroeder hardly charged anything for the wire. He says to tell you he's sorry about your jackrabbit."

We find a nice spot for the tortoise's new pen, an area with enough grass and weeds to keep him happy, and begin laying out boards.

"One-Eye will need shade," I say, straightening a corner into a better right angle, "but I suppose I can put something together out of cardboard or maybe fabric. Hand me the hammer, Nick?"

A voice behind me says, "That's not a girl's job."

I turn as someone who is almost Nick's double kneels beside me. Nick's double through the face and in how his shoulders look straight and strong, that is. Only his coloring is different: golden instead of red hair and freckles. Something thuds inside me, like one of those boards is slamming into my middle.

"I guess," I say, struggling to keep my voice level, "you're Boy Blackwell."

He nods, reaching for the hammer. "No job for a girl pretty as you, anyway," he says.

"Thank you for helping put out the fire last night."

"Hi" is all Nick says, and after that the two of them work on building the pen, though not exactly together.

Boy is unwrapping the wire when he notices the tag. "Schroeder?" he asks. "A Kraut place?"

A Kraut... for a moment I don't even realize what he's asking: if the lumberyard is owned by a German.

Nick realizes, though, saying shortly, "I guess Mr. Schroeder is mostly a Texan."

"And he's nice," I add.

Boy doesn't say more about it, though he looks at the tag again before tearing it off.

The chicken wire is rolled so tight he has a hard time getting it straight, and I try to help.

"Don't, Asia," Boy says. "You'll get scratched."

He anchors it with a board, moving my hands out of the way as he does. His own hands are large and rough, and they hold mine an instant more than right. "Just so I'll know," he asks, "are you anybody's girl?"

I don't know how to answer. I'm not, but Nick's here and so perhaps I'm not *exactly* not... but... I shake my head.

"Well," Boy says, "maybe we'll fix that."

"No one needs you to fix anything," Nick says, a rudeness in his voice that's not like Nick at all.

The two of them finish the pen with hardly another word. It is so uneasy, I'm plain glad when Boy says he guesses he'll be going.

After Boy leaves, I begin picking up spilled nails. "Nick," I ask, "don't you like your cousin?"

"Not particularly." Then Nick adds, "But, Asia, what I *do* like is how your hair shines in the sunlight."

This is so unexpected I can't think of any answer but

thank you. Then I stretch forward for a wood sliver just as Nick goes to pick it up, and our foreheads clonk together.

And, of course, at this moment my brother comes out and sees us. One glance and Homer is yelling out a chant at the top of his lungs:

> *Nick and Asia,*
> *Sitting on the ground,*
> *Kiss, kiss, kiss,*
> *Till love comes round.*

The screen opens. Grandmama reaches out, hooks Homer by his collar, and hauls him back inside.

I am so mortified I hardly dare glance at Nick. When I do, I see he's gathering tools, acting like he hasn't heard. But his neck and ears are bright red again.

3

SUPPER IS IN THE KITCHEN, early and silent after the day of fire talk that has led nowhere. Homer's keyed up, fidgety and not wanting to let the excitement go. Papa's spent the afternoon in his accounting office at the railroad depot, but instead of telling us what all is going on in town, he sits angrily still. Mama, passing around macaroni salad and a platter of cheese sandwiches, just looks tired.

I want to talk about Straw Bit, but I can't think what to say. And nobody, not even May or Grandmama, helps me out by bringing him up.

The doorbell rings as we're finishing. It's Nick and his folks, and behind them on the front porch is Boy Blackwell.

I see Mama flash Grandmama one quick look—not company, not tonight—and then she's moving everybody in, offering rice pudding and apologizing because it's not very sweet. A lot of our food is different than it was before the war began, because of the government making us save things like sugar and wheat flour so they can go to our soldiers.

Mr. Grissom's brought tomorrow morning's newspaper to show us a small story he's put on the second page. It says that Friday night a fire of unknown origin destroyed an outbuilding at the Chester McKinna residence.

"You haven't learned anything more about how it started?" Mr. Grissom asks.

Papa seems to hesitate before answering. "No. Probably some vagrant."

"But *why*?" I ask, the way I have at least a half dozen times without getting answered. "*Why* would a vagrant want to burn our chicken coop?"

Mrs. Grissom says, "Meanness."

Grandmama, turning to Boy, says, "I understand you're going to be staying with your aunt Nell and uncle Charlie awhile?"

"Until my father is better enough that Mother can bring him back home to Louisiana." Boy looks at me. "Father's a marine. He lost a leg fighting in France."

He's going to be living with the Grissoms? Why didn't Nick tell me that when I asked who Boy was?

As though he's caught my question, Mr. Grissom says, "Don't know what it's going to be like, two young bucks in one household. I hope they don't set their sights on the same young lady."

I'm thinking Boy and Nick are likely dying of embarrassment—what kind of way is that for Mr. Grissom to talk? And doesn't he even care about Boy's father?

Then I realize that Boy and Nick are both staring at me. They're thinking Mr. Grissom's talking about them and *me.*

And I guess, judging from how everybody else is looking my way, they all think so, too, except for Homer. He asks, "What bucks?"

"Hush," Mama tells him, abruptly standing up. "Shall we move outside?"

AS OUR FOLKS settle into chairs on the porch, Homer talks the rest of us into a game of hide-and-seek. He races down our twilit street rounding up others: the Crandall brothers, Chrissy Buxtrad, one of her friends.

"Not it!" Homer yells, just as an edge of moon cracks over a curve of horizon.

I wind up taking the first turn at home base, hiding my eyes against a telephone pole for the count. "Anyone around my base is it!" I holler, right away spotting May behind the screen porch.

I'm still trying to find people when Boy Blackwell runs in and frees everybody I've already got. And then he lopes off so slowly he's plain inviting me to tag him, which I do.

"Guess I'm caught," he says, a double meaning in both his words and his eyes.

And Nick, ready to slap the base, veers my way instead.

On and on we play in the moonlight, our yells cutting through the summerlike night.

Finally Mama calls, "You children be finishing up now."

Homer, about to be it again, pleads, "Just one more turn, please?"

I run for a last place to hide as he begins his count. I drop to the dust behind an oleander shrub and peer through the branches.

"Asia." Nick's whisper comes from several feet away. Then he's running swiftly, dropping to the ground beside me.

Homer whirls about. His look sweeps across the bush that hides us.

A wispy cloud shifts, and brighter moonlight suddenly makes the ground around us glisten and we see a snake's shed skin lying nearby. It sparkles silver and ghostly gray-white.

"Look, Nick," I whisper. "It even has the clear scales that covered the snake's eyes."

Nick moves closer, so close our arms touch. His face so near I can feel his breath. I know, suddenly, Nick is going to kiss me, and I'm not surprised when he does.

So this, I think, is what someone else's lips feel like. So *soft*.

Then Homer is off to our left, pelting toward base. "Asia and Nick behind the oleander bush," he yells.

I grab Nick's hand. "Come on."

We race my brother, slapping the telephone pole at the same moment he does. Our "all free"s drown out his "I beat you."

Boy runs in yelling, "Homer, you're slow." Then he

focuses in on Nick and me, and for an instant his eyes narrow.

May runs in next with a quiet "Free." Her glance flicks from one to another of us.

We all seem locked in a strange moment that doesn't end until Nick says, "I guess it's time to quit." Before he walks off he looks at me, a look that says we both know something has changed.

WHEN I GO OUT to use the privy a last time that night, I meet May coming from the house. "Asia," she says, "aren't you going to be glad when that new dam is finished and we can get city water and indoor plumbing?"

"At least we have electricity and phone lines. Some places out in the country, there's not even that."

We're both in our nightgowns and wrappers, white cotton flannel that shines in the moonlight. It reminds me of the snake skin, and on impulse I say, "May, come help me find something."

"Out front?" May asks, following. "Asia, we can't go along the street dressed like this."

"Shush. No one will see."

"Did you lose something?"

"No, it's just..." *Which oleander were we behind, Nick and me?* I have to walk clear to the telephone pole and look from there to figure it out. "...a snake skin I saw before."

Clouds hide the moon, and I search the ground by feel.

"Asia, whyever do you want a snake skin?"

"To remember. May...Nick *kissed* me."

My sister's gasp overlaps Mama's calling to us, "Girls? GIRLS? Where are you?"

Just then I find it. "Let's go, May," I say. "We'll talk later."

I put the delicate keepsake on the memory shelf in our bedroom, placing it between a seashell I got the time we went to Galveston and the singed tuft of Zoey's hair.

4

SUNDAY AFTERNOON Papa and the police chief are poking through the burnt debris again. They're calling the fire arson, a fire deliberately set by someone, but they're no closer to knowing who.

Chief Minette makes me repeat what I remember about that shape I thought might be a person.

"At first I thought it was Grandmama, since she'd gone out back. But she's so tiny..."

"So you saw a bigger person, Asia? Taller?"

"Maybe. I don't know. It was a shape. Just a dark shape."

Papa suddenly shakes his head as if he wants to be done with the whole thing. "I'll get Mr. Hawley and Zep Broom in tomorrow to clean up this mess."

THE NEXT DAY the scrapes and clangs of their shovels reach me as I hurry home, chilled by a raw wind so strong I have to fight my way backward into it. I find Mama and Grandmama at the kitchen table sorting garden seeds.

"Looks like winter has returned," Mama says.

"Just March being itself," Grandmama answers. "It's a wonder dirt's not blowing under those rattling windows. Asia, cut yourself some corn bread."

As I eat I watch the two of them. They work easily together, like they don't even hear the clatter coming from the back.

Finally I ask, "Doesn't that noise *bother* you?"

Mama looks up, puzzled. Then she asks, "Missing Straw Bit?"

And Grandmama reaches across the table to pat my hand. "Of course you feel low."

"I keep seeing Straw Bit in my mind," I tell them, "but the picture isn't the one I want. I need a *real* picture of the way he was—of how things were—*before*."

That's not exactly what I mean, but I don't know how to get closer. How to say, yes, I miss Straw Bit, but also I'm mixed up about Nick and Boy and I hate the racket outside and that the new chicken house is going to be bigger and have a different design than the old one.

Mama says, "A picture wouldn't bring Straw Bit back, Asia."

"You'll remember him," Grandmama says.

BOY FITS INTO Dust Crossing High like he's always belonged. It's because he's Nick's cousin, I guess.

I don't see much of them the next few days. They're always with the other seniors during school, and afterward they both have to be down at the *Sentinel*. Nick's got his job inside, and Boy's taking on a delivery route.

Still, a person would think...

"May," I ask at lunch Thursday, "is Nick avoiding me?"

"Probably," she says, "if you've been carrying on to him the way you have to me about what you see and what you don't see."

"I haven't been carrying on."

"You have. Ever since the fire you've been talking about wanting to keep things the way they look. You're going to wind up in the loony bin." She pauses to cut her sandwich. "Mind pictures! Asia, why can't you just have memories, like everybody else?"

"I do," I tell her.

But these are different, these moments that seem caught where only I can see them: the shape under the pecan tree the night of the fire... Straw Bit leaping... Nick, how he looked just before he kissed me. They're sharper-edged than memories; real and unchanging inside me.

Real and unchanging. *Not enough,* but the best I have.

"May, don't you ever want to think about something but you can't see exactly what it is that you want to think about?"

May tilts her head. "The loony bin if you're not careful, Asia."

A few minutes later, as we're walking to classes, I hear the clangs of the fire truck. Someone shouts, "There's a fire at the depot!" Then suddenly everybody's rushing outside.

The station ... where Papa's office is ...

Hurrying to the street, I expect to see smoke and flames shooting from the train station three blocks away, but I don't.

And when we get there and I'm out of breath and my side hurts from how fast I've run, there's still nothing much to see except one smoking barrel sitting in a thick scattering of sand. Long, scorched bags of sheep wool have been pulled every which way, and ticks of blackened straw are turning soggy in puddles of water.

Nick is already there with several other boys. They're kicking the straw apart; stabbing knives into the burlap bags and pulling out smoking hanks of oily fleece.

Straw Bit ... I hate fire. The thoughts seem to float in from nowhere.

Nick sees me and waves, pointing to Papa so I'll see he's safe.

My father is talking with Chief Minette and some other men: Mr. Grissom and Mr. Schroeder from the lumberyard and several I don't know. Boy Blackwell's with them, too.

At first the group is sort of huddled together, but gradually it changes shape until it's more a broken ring facing Mr. Schroeder. He's talking, gesturing, and even from my distance I can see how distressed he is.

Papa must see it, too, because he steps beside Mr. Schroeder and puts a hand on his shoulder.

Meanwhile, Nick and the others rake the last embers dead. Then Nick comes over to May and me, and a moment later Boy Blackwell does, too.

"What's up?" Nick asks him, nodding toward the men.

"Just questioning the Kraut," Boy says. "He was at the depot not long before the fire broke out."

"Boy," I say, "don't call Mr. Schroeder that."

"Ask me nicely, sugar," Boy says.

"And don't call Asia *sugar,*" Nick tells him.

They both look quickly angry.

"Oh, quit it," I tell them. "Don't either of you be silly."

THERE IS A THIRD FIRE. It's hardly anything, just a brushfire out of town a ways where a spur switches off the railroad's main line. Boy Blackwell, out delivering papers early Sunday morning, spots the smoke and gets help before it can rage into wildfire.

Papa hears more at work the next day and tells us about it at supper. He says the men who put out the fire found the rail switch set in a halfway position that could have caused a train to jump the tracks.

"It's a good thing the fire got people out there. If not . . ."

"But how did the switch get moved?" Mama asks. "It doesn't seem like a thing that could just happen."

"Maybe it was the Germans," Homer says. "That's what my teacher thinks, that maybe it was Germans trying to cause a train wreck. German *subatage.*"

"*Sabotage,*" Mama corrects him, before saying to Papa, "Chester, surely not."

Papa shrugs. "It does seem preposterous."

THEN, AS FAST AS FIRE has come to Dust Crossing, it seems to be gone. I'm glad, because I have other things to think about.

Like how fast things are changing between Nick and me.

One early April evening Nick comes up beside me as I look for a seat in the school auditorium. Mama's up ahead chatting with Mrs. Grissom, and May is with girl-friends.

"Do you really want to hear about war relief efforts?" Nick asks.

"Mama says I do."

"My mother, too. Come on, we can listen from outside."

"Nick, we shouldn't...well, from the vestibule, maybe."

We reach it just as the last arrivals go inside. Someone closes the auditorium doors, and Nick and I are left to ourselves. I suddenly realize that the lecture is not going to carry out here. Nick's ears are turning red, so I know he's feeling as self-conscious as I am.

Now what do we do? Talk about the display?

It's mainly war posters, drawings of soldiers in spiked helmets murdering terrified women. I've seen ones like them before, frightening paintings of terrible things.

Nick, though, says, "Asia, look here."

He's found a board with a half dozen photographs taken by a relief worker. The pictures are stark black and white, hardly softened by gray, and they make me want to stare inside them, see *past* them.

"It's strange, Nick," I say. "These don't show anything near so bad as the posters do, but at the same time what they do show is worse."

"Because they're real, I guess."

I move to the next panel and find myself looking at a photograph mounted all by itself, a picture of a girl about my age.

Her hair is straight and dark, her feet jut out silly, and her face is so serious. But it is a face... grown-up with war.

I can almost imagine that I'm her. Maybe it's because of her eyes. How the photograph shows her eyes, and her eyes show her feelings.

"Nick, look," I say. "This is what I've been talking about, something stopped so a person can think about it."

Nick studies the photograph with me. "I guess," he says. But then, in another moment, he says, "Asia, come outside for a bit. No one will miss us."

5

I CAN THINK all the day long about Nick. It's like he's become somebody new, and I want to spend all my time with him.

Only, between school and his work, Nick is not around all that much.

One Friday afternoon I see Boy fling the newspaper on our porch, and it reminds me how Nick used to have that job. Every *day* he'd come around with the paper, and I never gave it any mind.

I take the *Sentinel* into Grandmama's room, where I flop on the bed, yawning.

"Asia, be careful you don't break down the mattress edge," Grandmama says. "Oh, my, here's another story about how badly we need rain. The poor farmers." And then, "Are you tired, honey? Close your eyes and let me read the personal news items to you."

I know I should offer to read them to her to help save her eyes, but listening lets me think. My thoughts swing between a report of someone's visit to a sister in Dallas and a conversation I had with Julia Crawford and Chrissy Buxtrad the other day. Chrissy, who's only a freshman, said, "Asia, two beaux—you're being talked about."

"I don't know what *you're* talking about," I answered, but they just laughed, and Chrissy said, "Asia, remember, I was playing hide-and-seek, too!"

And May. Only this morning she told me that if I don't want Boy Blackwell for myself, she just might.

Grandmama reads about someone's new baby and about the Sullivan family entertaining relations from Montgomery, Alabama. "Highlighting the social activities will be an evening card party."

I guess I dozed off, because the next thing I know, Grandmama is saying, "Asia, I asked you a question."

"I'm sorry, Grandmama. What did you ask?"

"Who the Sullivans are. That name sounds familiar, but I can't seem to place it."

"They're the new couple we met at church the week before last. Grandmama, don't you remember?"

She looks puzzled. "No, I don't believe I do."

"They're from East Texas, like you. You talked to Mrs. Sullivan for ten minutes at least."

Grandmama shakes her head, making a little exasperated sound under her breath. "I suppose it will come to me," she says, and goes back to her reading.

The Senior Social is coming up, I remember. I wonder if Nick will invite me. But what if Boy does?

ON SATURDAY, A WARM DAY that again promises summer, May and I go downtown for sodas. It's pure coincidence that we reach the corner of Fannin and Houston Streets, where the *Sentinel* office is, just as Nick gets off work. Of course, he goes on to Peat's Pharmacy with us.

It seems half of Dust Crossing High is already there, having ice cream.

"Fountain or table?" Nick asks, but before I can answer, some seniors, including Boy, call us to join them. They're near a counter where several men are talking war news with Mr. Peat.

Mr. Peat's son left school last month to join the army. "The sooner we get our main force into the action in France, the sooner this war will end," he's saying. "Our Yanks know how to fight."

"My dad did his part already, getting wounded," Boy tells the kids we're with. "I wish he didn't want me in college this fall, because otherwise I'd go pay the Huns back for what they did to him."

Nick protests, "Boy..."

The sounds swirl around me. The phonograph plays "Over There." May and another girl talk about what key it's in and what guitar chords they'd need. "It's one everybody likes to sing," May says. Then one of the men with Mr. Peat lights a cigar, and a fan sends the heavy smoke my way.

Straw Bit...I don't know if it's the sudden thought of him or just the smoke that makes my throat tighten and tears threaten.

"I'll be right back," I say, heading for the door.

"Asia?" Nick calls after me.

Then I'm outside, gulping dusty air that smells of nothing but spring grass and honeysuckle.

The pharmacy door opens and Nick comes out. "Are you okay?"

I nod. "Just...all that smoke."

"It reminded you of Straw Bit? Would you like to walk around the square?"

We turn, and that's when I first see the camera.

It's on a glass shelf in the pharmacy's front window, just it and a small price card. KODAK AUTOGRAPHIC, THE POSTCARD CAMERA. $55.

It is all gleaming silver rings and pulled-out leather bellows; finely turned metal fittings; black-and-gold numbered dials. Down on one corner, a chrome-framed cube of glass and mirrors breaks sunlight into blue, green, red, and yellow: a burning spray of color that sears itself into my mind. I stand still, no more able to move than if my breath had been knocked out.

Everything about the camera is hard-edged and shining, and clean and certain, and, and... *beautiful....*

It's as beautiful as the photographs mounted behind it; one, a woman's portrait, another, the sharp-edged image of a girl cradling a puppy. *The way I used to hold Straw Bit.*

There's something different about these pictures; they're better—or maybe stronger—something different from the snapshots my parents and their friends take.

I read another, longer card. This one says the camera is the No. 3A Autographic Special. TAKE THE GUESSWORK

OUT OF FOCUSING WITH THE WORLD'S FIRST COUPLED
RANGE FINDER.

"It's pretty, isn't it, Nick?" I say, carefully, once I can
trust myself to speak normally.

"It's expensive," he answers.

ON THE FAR SIDE of the courthouse lawn, we sit on a
bench watching a scissortail pick insects from the air.
Each time the bird catches one, it stops, just *stops,* like
it's making a moment of flight hold still to be looked at.

A person could take a picture of a moment like that,
I think....

*Or take a picture that raises gooseflesh, like that one of
the girl in Europe.*

"You're awfully quiet," Nick says.

"I'm thinking about the camera in Mr. Peat's window.
Nick, wouldn't it be wonderful to own a thing like that?
You could take pictures of anything you wanted, and then
you'd have them."

"You can do that with your father's Brownie."

My father's Brownie is a grained-paper box, plain as
a sewing basket. Sure it can take pictures, but...

"But that wouldn't be the same," I answer Nick. "I
mean, just to *hold* something like that Autographic..."

I know I'm not making much sense, but before I can
bring my thoughts together I hear May calling "Here you
are!" and Homer launching into one of his chants.

> *Nick and Asia,*
> *Sweethearts in the park.*

*Don't they wish
That it was dark?*

"Homer, hush up," May says. "Behave."

ON THE WALK HOME Boy Blackwell and May talk a
blue streak. May is laughing and more sparkly than I've
ever seen her, and I know I ought to think about this.
She's my *younger* sister, if only by eleven months, and
he's ... Boy is ... what?

But I can't quite bring myself to care, not right now.
Not when I'm still seeing those gleaming rings and leather
bellows, the rainbow in the Autographic's glass.

As though he can read my mind, Nick asks, "Asia, are
you thinking about that camera?"

I just nod. There's no way I can tell him how it jolted
me.

How can I explain that Straw Bit and the fire, Grandmama so frail, the way Nick and the snake skin looked in
the moonlight ... and that photograph I saw of the girl in
Europe, like me but not ... that they're somehow related
to that lovely, shining camera?

I'm still groping for an answer when Nick asks, "So,
have you figured out where you're going to get fifty-five
dollars?"

"You don't think I'm crazy?"

"As a loon," he answers. "But don't let that stop you."

6

THAT EVENING, I tell my family, "The Autographic costs fifty-five dollars, but I already have seventeen, and I'll find some jobs tending children. You know Mrs. Sullivan's always asking."

"Asia," May says, "I thought you were saving some of that to buy a phonograph with me."

Homer says, "Fifty-five bucks for a *camera.*"

"And, Mama," I say, "that summer sport skirt you said I might have from Dillard's is three-twenty-nine, and a waist to go with it is a dollar-ninety-eight. I could do without..."

Papa says, "Asia, it takes me close to two weeks to earn fifty-five dollars. And you want to spend it on some gadget!"

"It's not a gadget. I want to learn to take pictures— *good* pictures—and this camera has the very newest things on it."

"I'll teach you to use the Brownie," Papa says.

"It wouldn't be the same."

"Why not?"

"Because..."

"Asia," Grandmama says, "I believe I have a couple of dresses that can use hemming. I'll pay you twenty-five cents each."

THERE'S A FIGHT in school the middle of the next week, a free-for-all in the boys' locker room. What I hear is that Otto Schroeder said something ugly to Boy Blackwell, though no one seems to know just what, and Boy punched him. And then somebody grabbed Boy, who hit whoever grabbed him, and the thing spread.

Everybody involved is suspended through Friday, including Boy and Nick.

Mrs. Grissom comes over late Wednesday with a loaf of gingerbread she made with melted butter-substitute, and she stays to talk to Mama.

"Oh, Sophie," she says, dabbing at her eyes with a handkerchief, "it does upset me when my menfolk argue."

"What were they arguing about?" I ask, putting aside for later consideration the notion of Nick and Boy as menfolk.

Mrs. Grissom answers, "Things, Asia, just things."

I'd like to ring Nick on the telephone and find out what things, but Mama won't let me.

I FINISH GRANDMAMA'S sewing that evening, and after school Thursday I take all my money to Peat's Pharmacy.

"Mr. Peat," I say, "I've come to ask if you'll please put your camera, the one out front, on hold. I have twenty-two dollars for a deposit and I'll bring the rest as soon as I can."

He pulls back the window curtain and reaches in. "Tell your father he can put it on account, Asia."

And then it's there, right in front of me. Even inside the store, without sunlight making it gleam of magic, the Autographic is beautiful.

I touch the smooth leather, then trace a metal track to the cube of glass. "What's this for?" I ask.

"That's the coupled range finder for accurate focusing. And this camera is outfitted with a fast lens and an excellent shutter. Your father's getting a fine piece of equipment."

"Actually," I say, "I'm the one buying it."

Mr. Peat bursts out laughing. "You, Asia? Honey, just learning how to work it would take more brains than could possibly be rattling around in your pretty little head."

The door opens and Boy Blackwell comes in carrying a stack of *Sentinel*s, which he takes to a back counter.

Mr. Peat, calling "What's the news from overseas?" returns the camera to the window.

I hold out my money. "Will you keep the camera for me?"

"Do your parents know what you're doing?"

"Yes, sir."

"Then, Asia, of course I will. But before you leave,

why not look around and see if you wouldn't like something else..."

WHAT WITH NICK AND BOY being suspended from school and Mr. Grissom's restricting them to the house when they're not working, I don't see Nick until Friday evening. Then he arrives at our place carrying a big bunch of hollyhock plants Mrs. Grissom's giving Mama.

I take him outside to dig some blackberry shoots Mama wants to send in return, which gives me a chance to ask about the locker room fight. "Nick, do you know what started it?"

"Boy making trouble."

"I heard Otto Schroeder said something ugly."

"Because Boy said every German in Texas ought to be under suspicion for disloyalty. Boy's crazy on the subject." Nick slices the shovel blade through a tangle of roots. "Other people are, too. Dad says Mr. Schroeder's lumberyard business has fallen way off."

"That doesn't seem fair. Mr. Schroeder's always doing something nice for somebody else or to help the town."

I wrap wet paper around the sprouting roots Nick hands me before I change the subject. "Nick, Mr. Peat's holding the Autographic for me until I can save the rest of what it costs. Though I don't think he really believes I can earn that much."

"Can you?"

"I think so. I've found three regular jobs helping tend children after school, and I've told everybody I'm free

Friday and Saturday nights. I get a dime an hour—fifteen cents if I do housework."

"Asia—thirty-three dollars—that'll be more than three hundred hours of work," Nick says.

Three hundred hours...

"Asia," Nick says, "there's a new motion picture at the Bijou. Would you like to go to the matinee tomorrow?"

Nick's inviting me out! I could about cry when I have to answer, "I'll be sitting with the Buxtrads' baby. Mrs. Buxtrad thinks Chrissy's too young."

"Or to the show tomorrow evening?"

"I've promised Mrs. Sullivan I'll help her."

"Well," he says, sounding disappointed, "maybe when you're not so busy."

7

THE NEXT FEW WEEKS, though, are filled with caring for little kids and doing odd jobs for Mama and Grandmama, and Nick hardly has time for me, anyway. He's off doing stuff with other seniors and taking exams and practicing for commencement.

The best part—and the worst—of the whole time is the Senior Social, which Nick does invite me to.

May hopes Boy will ask her, I know, and after thinking about that for a while, I kind of suggest the idea to Nick. Just in case he might want to mention it to Boy.

The next day Boy catches up to me in the school hall. He walks alongside just long enough to say, "I don't take second best."

And then he's gone, leaving me flaming with embarrassment for me and May both.

But, anyway: the social. It's wonderful because I'm with Nick and because Nick thinks I'm pretty in the new dress that Mama made me for a sixteenth-birthday gift.

It's white organdy embroidered with pale yellow rosebuds.

"Asia," Nick says when he picks me up, "I wish you already had your camera so I could use it to take your picture." And as we enter a school gymnasium bright with a canopy of streamers all in our national colors, he says, "I am so proud that you're my girl."

I think, *So I am. I am Nick's girl.*

But the social is awful, also, and that's because of Boy, who's come by himself. He puts his name in three places on my program, and when I'm not dancing with him his eyes follow my every step.

Our first dance is all right; he's even kind of fun to be with.

Our second, though, is one of the new fox-trots, and Boy pulls me in too close, close enough for me to smell he's been drinking alcohol.

When Boy comes up the third time, swaying and flushed, I've been dancing with Nick, who says, "No more."

I don't know if Nick means "Stop drinking" or "You're not going to dance with Asia again." Whatever he means, the next second the two of them are shoving each other and someone's fist flashes by.

Chaperones hurry over, and the principal makes Nick and Boy leave. Everybody stares at me like their bad behavior is my fault. And when I look down, I see there's a long tear in the skirt of my dress.

Someone must have telephoned my parents, because pretty soon Papa comes to walk me home.

MR. GRISSOM SHOWS UP at our house the next morning with Nick and Boy and stands while they apologize to me and also to my parents.

Nick looks miserable.

I can't pin down Boy's look. It's someplace between defiant and... *what?*

NICK AND BOY REALLY DO get punished this time: Mr. Grissom pulls them out of everything but school and work, right until commencement night.

I double up on caring for children and doing odd jobs for Mama. I help neighborhood ladies serve tea at their war effort committee meetings, and I wash up the dishes after. May complains that I'm hardly fun at all anymore. "Everybody's talking about you at school, Asia."

"Saying what?"

"That you were wrong to make trouble between cousins. And that you're crazy to be working all the time just for a camera."

"What do you tell them?"

"I stick up for you. But, Asia, sometimes I don't understand you myself."

IT SEEMS FOREVER COMING, but finally commencement night—freedom night for Nick—does arrive. My whole family goes to the exercises with the Grissoms.

We listen to the principal say, "I hope this will be the last of our wartime graduations. We've sent so many young men off to fight and asked so many wives and sisters to keep the home fires burning."

To one side of him is an American flag, and to the other, a service flag that the senior girls sewed. Its fields of red, for bravery, and white, for purity of spirit, hold a blue star for each Dust Crossing boy in the armed forces.

I wonder, when the girls were working on the flag, did they think which star was for which boy? Did they match them up to the lists in the school annual: *Seniors gone to service, Jed Herod, William Covington, Daniel Swan, Henry Wilburn; Juniors gone to service, J. B. Lancer, Thomas Barker...*

I can't help getting a lump in my throat. I know it's silly—Nick will go to college this fall, not war, and it will be years before—well, it's silly. But something turns over inside me.

Afterward there's a reception on the school's side lawn, punch and cookies under lanterns strung from tree to tree. People surround the graduates to offer congratulations.

I shake Boy's hand and then Nick's; they're together at the center of the biggest group. Nick asks, "May I walk you home later?" And when I nod he says, "I'll meet you out front."

THE PARTY GOES ON for another hour before people start to drift away. I wave at Nick and then slip around the corner of the school into the shadows of the front lawn.

The string quartet that's playing at the reception shifts

into a slow, final song. Its notes come faintly, carried to me by the gentlest breeze ever on a spring-summer night.

I close my eyes, thinking about Nick, imagining what the summer's going to be like with him. Maybe it's because of what the principal said, but somehow I feel older, feel *we* are older.

Footsteps sound behind me, and hands cover my eyes.

"Hi," I say. Eyes closed, I let myself be turned around and kissed.

"I was proud of you tonight," I try to say, but my words are smothered in a kiss that is long and different, one that takes me a moment to become part of. Then, remembering myself, I draw back. "Nick..."

Only, it's not Nick. It's Boy standing in front of me, hands still holding my shoulders, ready to kiss me again.

I'm so stunned I can't even move.

And while I'm standing there, standing so still that Boy thinks it's all right and he puts his mouth on mine again—that's when I see Nick. He's just a few feet away, stock-still, looking.

"Nick," I call, but already he's turning to leave.

I shake loose of Boy.

"Nick," I call again, and start after him.

But he's walking rapidly away, his back toward me, his body rigid.

"Nick," I call once more, but his steps don't slow.

"BUT, ASIA," MAY ASKS, "what did you do? About Boy?"

"Nothing."

"You didn't slap him? That's what you should have done."

It's the middle of the night, long after the rest of the house has gone to sleep. May and I have been whispering for hours over what happened.

"No. I just left," I answer.

Just left because there never was a time that seemed right for slapping. When I should have been fighting, I just stood there. And afterward, after I'd made such a spectacle of myself by pleading with Nick's retreating back, how could I?

"Oh, May," I say now, "do you think Nick will ever speak to me again?"

"Maybe, if you explain you got him and Boy mixed up."

"You don't think he'll be angry that I couldn't tell Boy's kiss from his?"

"Whose is better?" May asks.

"May!"

"Well?"

"And besides," I say, "what if Nick won't give me a chance to explain?"

8

NICK DOESN'T. Despite all my efforts, including waiting outside the *Sentinel* office for him to get off work. "If you'll just let me talk to you," I tell him.

"There's nothing to talk about," Nick answers. "What you do is your business."

SO THAT'S HOW the month of May ends. I'm out of school, out of a boyfriend, working all the time.

And I'm feeling really sorry for myself the afternoon I wander into Grandmama's room looking, I guess, for a little sympathy.

I find her sitting at the window, her frizzled gray hair showing thin in the slanting sunlight. "That you, child?" she asks, rising stiffly. "Here, help me face my chair around."

Then she goes to her desk and begins taking things from drawers. "Asia, will you write a couple of notes for me?"

When she holds out a pen, I see how the trembling in her hand is worse than usual. "Sure," I say, picking up a lined tablet. "Who first?"

"Your aunt Bertha. Just write, 'Dear Bertha, Have been thinking of how pretty your place must be this time of year and wishing I could—' "

"Grandmama," I say, "you don't mean Aunt Bertha? She died."

For a moment my grandmother looks confused, and then her face clears. "Did I say Bertha? I meant your aunt Carrie. Write, 'Dear Carrie,...' "

Outside, Boy Blackwell flings newspapers from a large canvas sack. One thumps on our porch.

Grandmama's going strong now, dictating Dust Crossing news to all our East Texas relatives. We've done four letters before she finally says, "Asia, thank you."

"You're welcome," I answer. "Would you like to see the *Sentinel*?"

I glance at the first pages as I carry it in. There's a large Peat's Pharmacy advertisement, including prices for Kodak film, and next to that a Dillard's notice of a sale on clothing for young men.

Without warning, my eyes fill with tears.

"Asia?"

"It's nothing," I answer. "It's just...I kind of miss Nick...and I've been doing so *much* work...and I'm nowhere close to getting my camera. Grandmama, did you ever want something so much you just ached?"

Grandmama doesn't answer for the longest time, just

stares at the four envelopes we've addressed. And then she says, "Asia, would you like to borrow the rest of what you need?"

I catch my breath. "Do you mean it? But I know Papa wouldn't like me to borrow."

"Maybe. Maybe not." She reaches for her pocketbook. "What your father doesn't know won't hurt him!"

THE NEXT DAY, as soon as I'm done watching Mrs. Sullivan's children, I go right to Mr. Peat's. "Change your mind yet?" he asks.

I answer by counting out, "Thirty-one, thirty-two, thirty-three... plus the twenty-two dollars I put down makes fifty-five dollars."

"Asia," he says, "you've surprised me."

And then, minutes later, I'm sitting at one of the fountain tables holding the Autographic, *my Autographic*.

I'm turning it around and over, trying to see everything about it, when the side-by-side planes of the range finder catch my face and reflect it back. It gives me the strangest feeling, as if the camera and I are somehow part of each other.

I'm startled from my thoughts by the door opening, Nick bringing an advertisement layout for Mr. Peat to approve.

"Nick," Mr. Peat calls, "go see what Asia's done bought herself."

"So you got it," Nick says, and for an instant his face lights up with pleasure for me.

And then the door opens again, Boy this time with the *Sentinel*s. "Hey, Mr. Peat," he shouts, "the Germans are almost to the Marne River."

"The Allies will stop them," Mr. Peat answers. "But I hear it's bloody fighting."

"Well, congratulations," Nick tells me, and I know, just from listening, how he looks: how his jaw's gone tight and his body tense again. "Enjoy the camera."

"I will."

AT HOME, May's all for trying out my camera right away. "Asia," she says, "you don't have to memorize every word of those instructions before you take a single picture."

"I don't want to break anything."

"You won't. What's this slot on the back for?"

"That's where you write whatever you want to say about your pictures." I unsnap a small metal stylus from its holder above the slot and flip open the slot's hinged cover. "Somehow, writing in here puts the words onto the film."

May pretends to write. "I'm saying 'Asia's first photograph.' Now, what are you going to take?"

"You," I answer, though I'm thinking that what I'd really like is a picture of Nick and me back together again.

I don't get either. Nick's not here, and long before I've figured out how to load a roll of film in the camera, my sister has lost patience and gone to find something else to do.

"Asia," Papa says the next morning, "you can't take a picture in the living room. There's not enough light."

"Asia," Mama says, "don't go taking my picture now. I look a mess."

"You could have built a house faster," Homer tells me.

"Go away," I answer, though of course he doesn't.

I think I've got everything set. Holding the camera carefully, waist level, I look down into the viewfinder that frames a picture of our house. Okay...

I press in the shutter release and hear a slidy sound begin just as Boy Blackwell appears with the newspapers. "Hey," he says, "whatcha doing?" as he crosses in front of me.

A couple of days later, I tear open a packet from Peat's Pharmacy, eager to see the pictures from my first roll of film. None are any better than that one of the house with Boy Blackwell a blur in the middle.

"Asia, it takes time to learn a new skill," Mama says, looking at the postcard-size prints I've spread on the table.

"You should have saved your money," Homer tells me. "Papa does better with the Brownie." Then he gives me this grin, part tease and part smirk. "Does Nick know what bad pictures you take?"

I haven't told my parents that Nick and I aren't seeing each other anymore, partly because they didn't officially know we were and partly because—well, I surely can't tell them about those kisses.

And I guess Nick hasn't mentioned anything at his house, either.

The result is that Mama accepts an invitation for my family to eat at the Grissoms' the second Saturday in June.

The whole meal through, Nick talks to Homer about how to build a pushcart. And then, as soon as we're done eating, the two of them take off to look at Nick's old one, May and Boy trailing along.

Because I stay inside I hear Mama ask Mrs. Grissom, "Nell, how is your brother doing?"

"About the same," Mrs. Grissom answers, shaking her head. "If he'd just listened back when this war started ... A wife and son at home, there was no call to volunteer. But he was set on it, and not so old the service wouldn't have him. Though just what he expected..." She takes a picture from an opened envelope and turns to me. "Boy's father."

I could guess who he is without being told, the likeness to Boy is so great. He's in a wheeled, wicker-backed chair. There's a blanket over his lap, but you can tell from its flatness that one of his legs is gone.

What's striking, though—or maybe not so much striking as just what I notice—are his eyes. They're looking just a bit away, as though he's avoiding the photographer's gaze. Eyes squinted tight at the corners, defiant and resentful and ... something else ... arrogant, maybe, but more....

Like Boy's eyes.

FROM OUTSIDE COME excited voices, May calling, "Not so fast, not so fast."

I hear running feet, the scritch of wheels on the Grissoms' drive, and then I see her go by in the cart, being pushed by Boy. "Boy," she calls, laughing, "not so fast!"

WE EXCHANGE ANGRY WHISPERS across the space between our beds.

"Asia, you're too hard on Boy."

"May, he's sneaky."

"Asia, you can't keep every boy in Dust Crossing for yourself."

"Every boy ... May, I don't have a single one."

"Well, that's your own doing. Asia, all I did was let Boy give me a pushcart ride."

"It's not safe."

"A pushcart ride?"

"No, May. I mean ... I don't trust Boy."

"Oh, fiddle. Because he kissed you? Asia, did you ever think you might have led him on?"

"May!"

"Well, did you?"

"Of course not."

Boy's as much a puzzle as the pecan tree, I think; it's as hard to figure him out as it is to put a face to the dark shape I saw under the tree the night of the fire.

There's something I know about Boy, something I've seen, but what? I am *so close,* but I can't quite think it out.

9

EACH AFTERNOON MAY changes into her new middy top, brushes her hair, and arranges herself in the porch swing in time to be there when Boy brings the paper.

"May," I tell her on the fourth day in a row she's done this, "you're being obvious."

"Sitting on my own front porch playing my guitar?"

"Hi, beautiful," Boy calls to her as he turns up our walk.

Since when, I think, doesn't he just throw the paper? Maybe I should have told May what he said about not settling for second best. Why did I ever think Boy was good-looking?

"I'll take it," I say.

In the kitchen Mama reads aloud the headlines, all war news and drought worries, while Grandmama cooks and Homer and I snack on corn bread dipped in buttermilk.

"Not much else," Mama says, turning to the second page. "More about the next Liberty Bond campaign.

Charlie Grissom's beginning a promotion down at the *Sentinel* for young people who want to start Thrift Cards."

My Grandmother's answer is a little explosion of breath, a sort of *chuchhhhh*.

I ask, "You don't think buying Thrift Stamps to save up for a War Savings Stamp is a good thing, Grandmama?"

She again makes that little exploding-her-breath sound. "Just like all those Liberty Loan drives. They're a way for the government to take hard-earned money from families that need it, and then the war ends and who's richer? The ground, maybe, someplace far away, with blood, and that's about all. The ground, and the Yankees, of course, they always come out richer."

For a moment I'm confused, since our side *is* the Yanks, Yanks going to save Europe from the Germans. Then I realize Grandmama's talking about *her* war, the one that was going on when she was a girl.

"You mean the War Between the States, don't you?"

Grandmama goes to the oven and thrusts her hand inside to check the heat. "Don't talk to me about war. Men going off expecting a good time and then they're surprised when they get shot up."

Mama presses her lips together. "Ella," she says to Grandmama, her voice quiet, "are you ready for the pan of biscuits?"

Homer, though, wants to talk about the war we're in right now. "My teacher said we have to stop the mailed fist—that's the Germans—from spilling the lifeblood of defenseless nations. And she said Germans *murder* American citizens on the high seas and—"

"That's enough, Homer," Mama tells him.

"Grandmama," I say, "this war is for a good reason. President Wilson says we need it to protect democracy."

Grandmama's answer is only another disbelieving *chuchhhhh*.

After supper I go to my father with what Grandmama said. "Papa," I ask, "why *are* we at war?"

"Because our friends—France and Great Britain—are at war, and friends support friends and help them stand up to bullies. And, also, I suppose, because when our friends are in danger, then the interests we have in common are also in jeopardy."

"But why did Germany and our friends in Europe get into a fight to start with?"

Papa takes several moments to think before he answers. "I guess, Asia, because they were set to. There were a lot of countries in Europe—Germany and the other Central Powers as well as our allies—all armed, making promises that if one went to war the next one would also. When you've got people—or countries—preparing for a fight, it doesn't take much to get it started."

Like Boy and Nick, I think. *Expecting to fight, so they do.*

"So ... do you think this war is a good thing?"

"Asia," Papa answers, "I think I have to trust my country to do what's right."

———

AND A LITTLE WHILE LATER, Grandmama calls me to her room, where I watch her count out three quarters.

"I want you and May to take these down to the *Sentinel* tomorrow," she tells me. "Start yourselves Thrift Cards and start one for Homer, too. I won't have people thinking this family does not know its duty."

She puts away her pocketbook. "You know, my father never did recover from his wound. It left him without much will."

"What do you mean?" I ask, but my grandmother seems to have drifted away someplace, the way I have seen her do once or twice before.

"Blood's thicker than water," she says. "You have to take care of your own."

MAY'S BUSY the next morning, so I go to the *Sentinel* office by myself. I was hoping Nick would be there to help me, but he's not in sight, and Mr. Grissom himself takes my money.

It's the first time I've been inside the office, and I look around at the cluttered tables and typewriting machine. There's a pungent, nose-wrinkling odor in the air, which Mr. Grissom says is printer's ink. "Best smell in the world."

Then he says, "Asia, you'll be interested in Sunday's picture page. It just came off the press."

Mostly it's photographs of soldiers dwarfed by their own artillery or running into fields of smoke. "Who takes these?" I ask.

"The Associated Press."

Underneath, beside a drawn advertisement for Dillard's summer dress sale, there's a photograph of Mr. Schroeder.

"Why are you putting Mr. Schroeder's picture in the paper?" I ask.

"He's promised to match the largest pledge any Dust Crossing man or woman makes at the National War Savings Day meeting coming up." An unhappy look crosses Mr. Grissom's face. "I doubt he can afford to, but I suppose it's his way to prove he's loyal."

ALL THE WAY HOME I keep thinking about the *Sentinel*, especially about that photograph page. So maybe the Associated Press has people whose job is just to take pictures of news.

And I think, too, about Mr. Schroeder. It must be awful always to have to struggle to prove who you are.

SUNDAY AFTERNOON I set my Autographic on the ground and open the instruction booklet. I'm going to photograph the pecan tree—once and for all move its picture from my mind to paper—and I'm determined to do it right. I just wish the shape I remember could be part of the picture.

I also wish I could figure out what dial the booklet means when it says *adjust the aperture.*

I'm trying to pretend I'm not even aware of Nick twenty feet away, helping his mother and Mama rig shade for a sun-and-wind–scalded bush. He's not here to visit me.

Just then, May and Boy half run around the side of the house. "Asia, Nick," May calls, "there's an airplane landed in a field past where the new dam's being built. Do you want to go see?"

Walking all the way out there and back—maybe I can finally get Nick to listen. I start to answer, "Sure," but then I hear Nick say, "No. I'm busy."

Mama throws a sympathetic glance my way—*Does everybody read my mind?*—and says, "Nick, your mother and I can finish this."

"I'll do it," he says.

The only reason I know he's aware of me—that he's saying he doesn't want to walk out there with *me*—is because his ears are red. So I don't need him.

And I guess I don't need to see an airplane close up, either. I couldn't even photograph it, not when I can't work my camera.

Whatever is a danged aperture?

10

I'M THINKING AGAIN about the newspaper office when I realize the Associated Press probably did not take Mr. Schroeder's picture. Mr. Grissom, when I go to the *Sentinel* Monday to ask who did, tells me he got it from Mr. Riley.

"You mean from the portrait studio? Is he a good photographer?" I ask.

"The best in Dust Crossing."

Leaving, I almost bump into Nick coming in. There's a surprised instant, and I use it to say, "Nick, if you don't want to listen to me, then you should talk to Boy, because what happened was his doing. Though I'd be surprised if he'd tell you the truth."

Relief—or maybe hope—relaxes Nick's face for an instant. *He wants our disagreement to end as much as I do.* But then those jaw muscles tighten back up.

"I know what I saw," he says.

MR. RILEY'S PLACE is a block back from the courthouse square in a row of small houses that have businesses in their downstairs. There's Mrs. Heath's Tailoring and Handwork, a shoe repair shop, then Mr. Riley's Photographic Studio.

Framed portraits fill the window of a cool, shady parlor, and a sharp, sweet-sour mix of smells hangs over everything. A man calls, "Be with you in a minute."

Then Mr. Riley comes out from behind a curtained-off room. "Just mixing chemicals," he says, untying a black rubber apron. "What can I do for you?"

"I'd like to learn to take pictures."

He smiles. "I'm sorry. This isn't a school."

"I know." I begin again. "I'm Asia McKinna. I've got a Kodak Autographic—"

"The one with that coupled range finder device?"

"Yes, sir. The 3A Special. But, the problem is, I don't understand the instructions and nobody I know does, and, well...I was wondering if perhaps you would explain them to me, and maybe help me get started. I could work for you in exchange."

I can see that Mr. Riley is going to say no.

"Please," I say, rushing, "I can't pay you, because I'm still paying back money I've borrowed to buy the camera, but I'll do whatever you need, help write up orders....or mix chemicals...or...." I look around the parlor. "Or dust."

"Miss McKinna," Mr. Riley says, "it takes a long time to learn to use a camera properly."

He's busying about, moving things on the counter and straightening a wall picture, not wanting, I realize, to have to look at me when he refuses. He picks up a fishing pole and props it in a corner. "Don't know why I keep this around when I never have time to use it." Then his hand goes back to the pole.

"Asia," he asks, "do you think you could wait on customers if I weren't here? Set up appointments and take in film for processing?"

"Of course," I answer. *Anything.* "I'm sure I could."

"Well, then," he says, "I'll tell you. You check with your folks... You're Chester McKinna's daughter?"

"Yes, sir."

"If it's okay with them, I'll try you out. You mind my studio for a couple of hours every day to give me some fishing time, and I'll teach you what I can about photography. No wages, but I'll give you film when you need it and you can develop it yourself for free."

I can hardly believe my ears, it is so much more than I'd hoped for.

"An apprentice," I burst out, dragging the word from a history lesson. "I'm going to be your apprentice."

Mr. Riley's smile broadens, and he seems to consult his fishing pole. "Well, Asia McKinna, maybe you are."

"ABSOLUTELY NOT," Papa says. He turns to my mother. "Sophie! What put such a notion in Asia's head? You talk to her."

"Asia," Mama says, "you just can't work in a man's business like that. It's not suitable."

"Why not?"

Homer stops sopping a roll in gravy long enough to say, "Asia, don't you know anything? You're a girl, dummy."

"And so what if I am? I bet I can mind his studio better than some boy would."

"Asia," Mama tells me, "that's not the point. It's just not proper for a young girl to work in a man's shop all alone. And don't say *bet*."

"People would talk," May adds, her voice soft and her face troubled.

"But," I argue, "if I'm going to take good pictures, I need to learn how. Mr. Riley will teach me."

"Asia!" My father is losing patience. "I don't want to hear any more of this nonsense."

Grandmama hasn't said anything so far, but now she puts her knife and fork on her plate and places her hands in her lap. "I'll go to Mr. Riley's with Asia," she says. "No one will talk if I stay in the shop with her."

Papa throws up his hands, exasperated, and Mama says, "Ella, you can't do that. It would be too much for you."

Grandmama says, "Don't tell me what's too much."

And that settles that. I, Asia McKinna, all of a sudden am apprentice to a photographer.

"THIS IS CRAZY," May says as we get ready for bed. "People don't have apprentices anymore. And never girls.

And, besides, apprentices were kids learning how to make a living at something. You're not going to make a living with your camera."

"Why not?" I snap, more to argue than anything.

But I edge into sleep imagining myself with my camera, photographing soldiers who do not care one way or another who I kiss. *Why not?*

11

MR. AND MRS. GRISSOM COME OVER Saturday evening so Mr. Grissom and Papa can work on the details of our annual fishing and camping trip, even though it won't be until the end of August. "Half the fun is planning," Papa says. "Where do you think we should go this year?"

"If we head south," Mrs. Grissom says, "there's a nice couple who might join us. We've heard of a good spot along the Pecos River."

Boy has come along. Without even a glance my way, he invites May for a walk. *Is that a bruise on his forehead?*

I don't know where Nick is. *So what?* I ask myself. *He's not my business anyway.*

At least I have my camera.

MONDAY MORNING I WAKE UP thinking *today.* This is the day I begin work.

I race through my morning chores, even though I'm

not due at Mr. Riley's until after lunch. Then I get the Autographic to try once more to figure out all I can on my own.

"Asia," Grandmama says, coming into the kitchen, "will you give the hall rugs a good beating?"

"I don't think they need it, not again so soon." *What do those numbers mean?*

"Don't argue with me." Grandmama's voice is sharp.

"I wasn't arguing, Grandmama." *Why such odd numbers?* "But don't you remember that Homer just did them a few days ago?"

"Don't tell me what I remember."

Mama comes in saying, "The Red Cross ladies are having lunch after our work session today, so you all eat without me."

"Mama, Grandmama wants me to beat the hall rugs. Didn't Homer just do them?"

"Thursday afternoon, I believe." Mama turns to Grandmama. "Ella, I'm sure those carpets don't need working on again so soon."

My grandmother walks past us to the pantry, her back stiff and her jaw set, as Mrs. Grissom appears at the screen door calling, "Ready, Sophie?"

After Mama leaves it's several long minutes before Grandmama comes out of the pantry carrying the makings to bake something.

"I didn't mean to argue," I tell her. "I'm sorry."

"I wouldn't have talked to my elders that way when I

was a child." My grandmother's gestures are jerky as she sets out the breadboard and rolling pin.

I watch for a moment, uncertain, before asking, "Are you still coming to Mr. Riley's with me this afternoon?"

"Certainly. I said I would, didn't I?"

WHATEVER WAS WRONG in the morning, Grandmama apparently has either forgotten or forgiven by the time we set off for Mr. Riley's. The closer we get, the more eager I become, until it's all I can do to match my pace to hers, to keep the hand I hold under her elbow from pulling her along.

Mr. Riley seems a bit surprised that I've shown up, but glad, and he's delighted to learn that my grandmother will be coming with me each day.

"Excellent, Mrs. McKinna," he tells her. "I'll be honored to have you here."

Within minutes they've positioned a chair at the parlor window, where Grandmama can work on her crocheting. "Now," Mr. Riley says, "I'll show Asia about. Just call if you need anything."

Grandmama nods. "Please don't worry about me."

And, truly, I don't think we give her another thought. Mr. Riley, once he starts explaining equipment to me, seems like a teacher who has been just waiting for a student.

The studio itself, the part where he actually takes pictures, is a long room that runs across the back of the house. The outside wall is mostly one great, tilted-in window so tall the ceiling has been cut away for its top. Huge, lightly frosted panes, five across and five down, diffuse into haziness the lines of a tree outside.

Mr. Riley smiles at my surprise. "I picked this house because it had a spot for a skylight."

In the middle of the studio is the largest camera I've ever seen. "That's what I use to take portraits," Mr. Riley tells me as I walk around the wood case and examine the huge, brass-barreled lens.

"Why is it so big?"

"To hold large sheets of film. That's how we get portrait-size prints."

Next we go into the darkroom, which isn't dark at all, because of an electric light overhead. Overflowing water sheets down the sides of a square black tank sitting in a long sink.

"This film should be washed by now." Mr. Riley picks up one of several thin metal frames hanging crosswise in the tank and clips it to an overhead wire. "Want to hang up those other negatives, Asia?"

MY WORKING HOURS are to be 1:00 to 4:00, weekday afternoons. When Grandmama and I leave Mr. Riley's that first day, Nick is waiting out on the sidewalk.

I'm so surprised I blurt, "What are you doing here?"

"I thought . . . I heard you were going to start here and I'd like . . ."

Nick's face, which for a moment looked just like it used to, turns annoyed, and his ears redden. "Oh, never mind."

"Nick," I begin, "I didn't mean...that is, I'm glad you came to..."

But Nick tells Grandmama, "Excuse me, Mrs. McKinna. I've got to get back to work," and then he's just *gone* again.

"Oh, Grandmama," I say, "why is he so touchy?"

"Asia," she answers, "sometimes you don't have the sense God gives a goose."

AT DINNER THAT NIGHT I try to tell my family every detail about Mr. Riley's. "A photography studio is so wonderful, you can't imagine. And there's so much to remember."

Homer goes into a great act of sniffing the air and wrinkling his nose. "What stinks?" He grabs my hand and holds it to his nose. "Asia, it's you. Asia stinks!"

"Homer!" Papa begins. "Apologize to your sister."

"Homer!" Mama says at the same time. "Don't say *stink.*"

"She does," Homer insists. "Her hand smells awful."

"Really," I say, pulling free. "That aroma is to be expected when one works with photographic chemicals."

"You were handling chemicals?" Papa asks. "Asia?"

And then, of course, I have to explain not really, they were just developing and fixing solutions.

"You actually developed pictures?" Mama asks. "On your first day?"

"Well . . . more like . . . I washed the tanks."

Homer bends so far over with fake laughter he gets mashed potatoes in his hair. "Asia's big career, she's washing dishes."

12

THE FOLLOWING EVENING is a town sing-along at the bandstand on the courthouse lawn. It's to support the war effort, but it's also a nice chance to visit.

I'm wondering if Mr. and Mrs. Grissom are coming and if Nick will be with them when suddenly he's next to me. He doesn't say anything, and he certainly doesn't take my hand, but he's there.

Asia, I tell myself, don't let on how much you've missed him. Just act natural....

I turn to say something to May, but she's disappeared. And then I glimpse her pink dress. She's slipping away from the crowd with Boy.

It makes me uneasy enough—May should know better—that I consider going after her. Just then, though, the band swings into "The Star-Spangled Banner," and I don't have any choice but to be still, hand over my heart. And besides, how can I leave Nick, now that he's finally come my way?

As we sing the last words—"...and the home of the brave..."—the mayor climbs to the platform to urge every Dust Crossing resident to do his or her part to back up our fighting men. "Don't be slackers," he says. "There is no more place here for slackers than there is a place for cowards on a battlefield."

Nick quietly adds, "Or anywhere."

THE DIFFERENCE BETWEEN farmworkers and May and me is that farmworkers get paid.

We're in the garden the next morning fighting the everlasting johnsongrass while Grandmama stakes tomato vines.

A grass blade slices my finger, drawing a line of blood. "Ouch," I exclaim. "Dang."

"Careful, child," Grandmama says. "Don't pull out the okra with the weeds."

Far across Mr. Lockett's cotton field, which butts up to our backyard, a cloud of dust traces the slow progress of a mule-drawn wagon. It's followed by the tiny figures of Mr. Lockett's kids working the rows.

"Grandmama," May asks, "did you ever hoe cotton? Back in East Texas?"

Grandmama moves to another plant. "When I was a girl, of course, and later on with your grandfather. Everybody in the family helped out when we had to. Chopped cotton and filled cotton sacks and got after boll weevils, too, every way we could."

She glances my way. "And," she adds, "I wore a bonnet to protect my complexion."

After a bit, done with the tomatoes, Grandmama goes to the barbed wire fence across the back. She stands there, staring across a long stretch of parched field covered with straggly plants.

What is she thinking? Maybe of all her years of work on the farm back in East Texas and how she hated to sell her part when Grandpa died? Of the good or the bad?

She looks both tiny and strong against that huge, impossible cotton field.

I brush off my hands, get my camera, and take her picture as best and as quietly as I can.

I SHOULD HAVE LISTENED about protecting myself from the sun. I don't know which is worse: how burned and freckled my face looks when we finally go inside or how it stings when May pats on lemon juice.

"That hurts!" I tell her.

"You better hope it bleaches," she says. "Do you want Nick to see you looking like a farmhand?"

"He wouldn't care."

"Boy would, if it were me all red and ugly."

"May...I wish..."

"What, Asia?" she demands. "That I wouldn't go around with Boy? He's explained about commencement night. He says he thought you knew it was him, and, anyway, he hardly knew me then. He says..." May looks to see how I'll take this. "He says he's got the sisters straight now."

"May, at the sing-along last evening—you and Boy were gone for almost the whole thing."

"So? Boy wanted to tell about how his father got hurt. Asia, Mr. Blackwell was running across no-man's-land all by himself, trying to rescue a wounded comrade. It's a lot for Boy to live up to."

"Mama and Papa wouldn't like you going off alone with him at night."

"You're not going to tell?"

"No, of course not."

"Besides," May says, "you were with Nick."

"We didn't leave the sing-along," I tell her. "And besides, it's different with us."

Way too different, I think. I wonder if things will ever be completely easy between Nick and me again.

MR. RILEY AND GRANDMAMA and I quickly get into a routine at the photography studio. The only thing I don't like is how fast it comes time to leave each day. Much sooner than I'm ready to go.

As my second week begins, Mr. Riley assigns me a few tasks, straightening and loading film holders and the like. Then he leaves with his fishing pole, Grandmama takes up her crocheting, and I go to work.

At three o'clock he returns.

"Did you catch anything, Mr. Riley?" Grandmama asks.

He shakes his head. "Not today."

The next hour is my apprentice time, when Mr. Riley teaches me about photography. Today's lesson is on cameras.

"They all work the same way," Mr. Riley says. "Each

is a box with a hole on one side that lets light through to film on the other. Here, look at the portrait camera."

He points to its large lens. "The light rays are gathered through here and projected to the viewing screen or film at the back." He steps to the parlor. "Mrs. McKinna, would you please help us?"

Grandmama sits in front of the skylight, a large white screen reflecting light to the shadowed side of her face. Mr. Riley motions me to duck under the black cloth at the camera's back.

At first I can't make out what I'm seeing, just a blur on milky glass. "Turn the wheel by your hand," Mr. Riley says.

Wood and leather creak as the camera's bellows extend and the front of the camera moves forward. The image becomes even more fuzzy.

"Other way, Asia."

Slowly my grandmother comes into soft focus. . . . "She's upside down!"

"And backward," Mr. Riley says. "The light rays converge as they come into the lens and are reversed as they leave."

I stick my head out to look at Grandmama, then back under the cloth to look at her upside down again.

"And what else?" I ask. "How does the rest of the camera work?"

Mr. Riley slides a film holder into place.

"Just light-sensitive film to record whatever image is projected onto it and a shutter to control when."

He pulls out the film holder's light-tight cover and

reaches for a squeeze bulb that dangles from the camera's side. "Shutter release, Asia...Smile, Mrs. McKinna.

"My prettiest subject today," he adds, and, honestly, Grandmama flirts back.

"Why, thank you, Mr. Riley," she says.

For the life of me, I don't know how she manages to look both down at her lap and up at him at the same time.

13

BOY GETS INTO ANOTHER FIGHT with Mr. Schroeder's son the first week in July, this time during the Independence Day parade.

I don't find out about it, though, until the next morning, when May and I go to town with a stack of magazines for a troop train. We see Boy painting someone's porch steps, working angry-like.

"What's the matter with him now?" I ask.

"Mr. Grissom's making him earn money to replace Otto Schroeder's glasses and Boy shouldn't have to," May answers. "It was a fair-and-square fight."

Those are Boy's words my sister's saying.

"What were they fighting about?" I ask.

"Otto was making treasonous remarks."

"And it was Boy's job to stop him?"

"Yes. Nick or anybody else would have."

"But, May . . . Boy takes the war so *personally.*"

"Well, he has a right to."

NICK IS AT THE DEPOT helping his mother sort and bind stacks of donated magazines and books. We talk a bit, but it feels stilted, as awkward as we were at the sing-along.

"Nick," I try saying, "May and I are going to the new picture at the Bijou." *Please say you'd like to come along.*

"I hope you have a good time," Nick tells me.

IT'S GRANDMAMA who brings Nick and me really together again, but not in any way I'd have wanted.

It comes about when finally, after only practicing film developing with scrap film and my eyes closed, I get to try it for real.

For days I've been learning how. I know what all the tanks of liquid are for: developer to bring up the image; a water bath to stop the developer; fixer to make the image permanent; more water for washing.

I've memorized the place of every last thing in the darkroom so that I can work without any light, even a safelight that accidentally might fog the film.

I've gotten to where I can count seconds as accurately as a clock's sweep hand.

Now Mr. Riley picks up his fishing pole and says, "Good luck."

"But . . . aren't you going to help?"

"You don't need me. You'll do a fine job."

"But what if I ruin—"

"Asia, do you want to learn this business or not?"

I explain to Grandmama what I am going to do. "I'll

be in the darkroom and I can't come out once I get started. You won't mind watching things out here?"

"I'll be happy to, Asia," Grandmama says. "You take your time."

WITH THE DARKROOM'S outer curtain and door closed, I make a last check for the equipment I'll need. *Light off.*

For a moment the black is so total I feel disoriented. But I tell myself: *One step at a time, Asia. Take it one step at a time.*

I feel for the film, trying to picture what my fingers are touching. *Where is...there...* I unwind a piece of string, then begin unrolling the film itself, freeing it from its double-layered paper backing.

Then, holding the film by the ends, picturing the length of it drooping into a stiff U, I move to the sink. With my elbow I find the left-most tank, the one with developer.

Slowly and steadily I begin the seesaw motion of pulling the film back and forth through the liquid. My eyes are open now, staring into the dark, imagining the lengthening and shortening legs of the U.

"One thousand and one," I count, "one thousand and two..."

I'm developing my own roll of film, turning film into negatives! I have this sudden thought that I am doing for the first time something that I will do many, many times again.

"...one thousand fifteen, one thousand sixteen..."

"Asia!" Grandmama's voice startles me. "Asia," she demands, "come out here!"

She's fumbling with the outer curtain, trying to find the door handle.

"Don't, Grandmama," I call. "Don't! You'll ruin my film."

"Asia, are you all right? Open this door!"

I make myself speak calmly. "Grandmama, I'm fine. I'm developing film and need the door closed to keep it dark. I'll be out in less than fifteen minutes."

There's silence. Then Grandmama's solid heels click away.

At first I feel relieved, but only until I realize I've lost count of the time. For how long? Half a minute maybe? A little less?

I can hear Mr. Riley saying, "Time in the developer is crucial, Asia. You must be as exact as possible."

I start in again: "Two thousand and one, two thousand and two..."

My first roll will not be exact.

"GRANDMAMA," I CALL, crossing the studio, "I'm done. Grandmama?"

"Grandmama?" I repeat as I step into the empty parlor.

14

MAYBE, I THINK, she stepped out on a quick errand.

But it wouldn't be like my grandmother to leave the photographic studio untended, not when she said she would watch things. Except ... she must have.

I put out the CLOSED sign and go looking for her.

I try the dry goods store first. Mr. Dillard, who is out front cranking down an awning, says, "No, Mrs. McKinna hasn't been by."

Mr. Peat hasn't seen her, nor has the postmaster. I look in the grocer's, the café, two meat stores. I even call to Mr. Higgins, driving the street-sprinkler wagon. "No, I haven't seen your grandmother," he says.

Maybe she's at the Sentinel, *gone to pay on the Thrift Cards.* Nick sees me at the door and comes over.

I explain. "Nick, I'm getting worried."

"Have you tried your house?" he asks.

"Not yet."

"You do that and I'll look some more around town,"

he says. "Maybe check the east side and down toward the creek."

"Nick..."

"Asia, she's probably at home. You look there."

BUT GRANDMAMA ISN'T HOME. The house is empty when I get there: Mama, May, and Homer are all off somewhere.

I run out back to check the privy and the garden, glance toward One-Eye's pen, look inside the new chicken house. Mama's bantam chicks, noisy anyway, raise their cheeping to a demanding racket.

I'm by the side of the house, trying to think where to look next, when I hear May call, "Asia!"

She and Grandmama are coming up the street, Grandmama carrying a small basket.

"Asia," May calls again, her words reaching me before I can say anything, "see what Grandmama has for us."

Grandmama lifts a napkin to show me a stack of tamales. Their spicy, corn-husk smell floats up. "A gift from Mrs. Mendosa," she says. "I went down to see if she might help us with the canning again this summer."

"Why did you...?" I begin.

But Grandmama is telling May, "Thank you for walking me home, child," and May is saying, "I only walked you the last two blocks."

I follow my grandmother into the kitchen.

"You frightened me," I tell her. "Why did you leave Mr. Riley's without saying something?"

Confusion crosses her face then. She seems so vulnerable.

And still I say, accusing, "Grandmama, you went all the way to Mrs. Mendosa's! That's clear past the icehouse."

"I did? Would you like something cold to drink, Asia?"

"Grandmama," and I can hear my voice getting shrill, "you didn't have any business going across town."

"Maybe I did and maybe I didn't."

"You could have fallen and injured yourself. Or gotten lost." I'm angry, suddenly full of anger that makes me want to hurt. Anger that says, Tell her how much she scared you, Asia. *Tell her.*

"Lost?" Grandmama says. "In Dust Crossing?"

She clanks down a plate so hard I'm surprised it doesn't crack.

"Asia," Grandmama says, crossing to the cupboard and taking out a red souvenir glass, the one etched in script *World Exposition, 1893.* She puts it in my hand.

"My sister and I went by ourselves to Chicago for that fair and we didn't get lost. We took the train all the way from Texas, stayed in a hotel, went every day to the exposition and we did not get lost one time. And you're telling me I might lose my way in this piddling little place?"

"You were younger then, Grandmama."

"I was forty-five!"

"And now you're seventy!"

The words are making themselves said, and I can't halt them. "You're old now; you just can't *do* things like that."

"Don't tell me what I can't do, young lady."

Grandmama presses her lips into thin, blue-white lines.

We stand, angry with each other, our voices ready to cut again with frightened edges. I know we are both thinking of the only rule we have to go on for such a time: Be proud and keep your backbone straight. Especially when you're afraid, keep your backbone straight.

I FIND NICK HURRYING along Fannin Street and tell him Grandmama is all right. "May brought her home."

"I'm glad, Asia," he says, squeezing my hand.

"But, Nick..."

The courthouse clock bongs three times. *The studio.*

"Nick, I've got to go, but... will you come by tonight?"

I reach the door with its CLOSED sign just as Mr. Riley does, and he looks from it to me.

"Grandmama felt ill," I say. "She needed to go home."

If Mr. Riley wonders, and I think he must, he doesn't question me further.

Inside, I finish washing my film, standing over it when I don't need to, soothed by the sight and sound of water flowing gently down the tank's sides.

Mr. Riley finally comes in and turns off the tap. "Let's

find out what you've got," he says, holding the long strip of negatives up to the light.

I crane my neck, anxious to see pictures I've taken and developed all by myself.

"That looks interesting, that backlighted one," Mr. Riley says. "How did you figure the exposure?"

"I . . . just guessed."

"Thought as much," he says, moving the strip along so we can view frame after frame. Several are muddy-dark and a couple almost transparent. "I guess our next lesson better be on camera settings."

I PUT OFF GOING HOME as long as I can, dreading having to face Grandmama, having to talk to her with an argument lying between us.

When I do get there, though, I find her going about the kitchen chores as if the day hasn't been anything unusual.

And Nick does come over after dinner, knocking at the front door and asking my father if he can please see me. He's never been quite so formal before, and it raises eyebrows in the kitchen.

"Run a comb through your hair," Grandmama says as I start out. "And straighten your collar."

I hear her say to Mama, "Such a nice young man," and Mama answer, "Asia's not a little girl anymore, is she?"

Nick and I walk a long time, looking at a new Franklin touring car a couple of blocks over, at the windows of closed stores, at a Bijou poster for *Say! Young Fellow,* starring Douglas Fairbanks.

"Nick," I say once, "about commencement night. I thought Boy was you and—"

"Asia, forget it," Nick answers. "It's handled."

"Well, anyway, I've had a lot of time to work. I've paid Grandmama back a lot of what I owe her."

We return to my house before either of us speaks about my grandmother again. Then, as we sit with our backs against One-Eye's pen, I say, "Thanks for helping today, Nick. Grandmama really scared me."

I pause, gathering thoughts I haven't voiced to anyone, hardly even to myself. "Something's going wrong with her, Nick, and I don't know what to do."

Nick puts his arm around my shoulders, a little clumsily, as though he wants to make me feel better but doesn't know quite how. "I'm sorry, Asia. Did you tell your parents she wandered off?"

"No."

A while later I say, "Nick . . . I don't want her to change. I don't want anything to change, not ever."

Which is when Homer finds us. "Gee, you two really are mushy." He circles, beginning one of his "Nick and Asia" chants.

"Homer," Nick says, "you go on now." Says it so quietly and firmly that Homer stops midsentence.

"You two aren't fun anymore," he mutters. "I'm not ever going to get stupid over any girl."

Nick and I stay with One-Eye a while longer, Nick's arm around me.

15

NICK AND I PICK UP as though that kiss that shouldn't have happened didn't. And one afternoon when Boy comes to call on May, he tells me, "Asia, I want to say I'm sorry."

"What for?"

"For getting out of line at graduation." He looks really contrite. "I don't know what I was thinking."

"Forget it," I say.

He looks sincere. I'd like to think so, for May's sake.

Anyway, with Boy's apology, he and May and Nick and I finally begin the kind of summer I've wanted.

We go places, to the picture show and out to watch work on the new dam, for sodas down at Mr. Peat's and for picnics by the creek.

And when I'm not with Nick, I have my camera and the photography studio and my neighborhood jobs. At least once a day, I think I have never in my whole life been so happy.

Even the war stays at a distance: For a time no one I

know goes off to join it, despite how the newspaper says we've got a million men in France and maybe we'll soon have two or three million.

And if Grandmama occasionally says something a little troubling—a few words that don't quite make sense—it's never enough to cause real worry. Like when a man over in Fort Worth is arrested for burning down his own business, and Grandmama says, "I'm glad that's finally settled." It takes us a bit to figure out she's thinking the person who set fire to our chicken house has finally been caught.

When we explain she says, "I better clean my ears."

MR. RILEY GIVES ME that lesson in camera settings—several, actually—and I learn, at last, about apertures.

"Watch," he says, opening the camera back so I can see the lens from inside.

He clicks the pointer along the dial of aperture settings, from $f45$ to $f6.3$. With each click the black-sided mask that surrounds the lens opens more.

"It's all mathematics," Mr. Riley says. "You double the amount of light you let in each time you open up the aperture one stop."

The other part of exposure is shutter speed, those *50, 100, 200* markings that mean $1/50$, $1/100$, $1/200$. Those are fractions of a *second*.

"Halve how long the shutter stays open and you halve the light that reaches the film, Asia," he says.

So shutter and aperture work together in a doubling,

halving way. It's a slippery concept, but Mr. Riley tells me I'll get it. "Think, practice, and use that Autographic writing stylus to keep track of what you do, Asia, and it will become second nature."

He doesn't fuss about how much film I use. Only when I don't use enough, only when I don't take every picture three times. "Do it the first time, Asia, at the exposure you've worked out, and twice more at exposures on each side."

GRADUALLY I BECOME more confident with my camera, which I begin taking with me everywhere.

In fact, once, when the fellows have come to take May and me to a band concert, Nick asks, "Are the three of you ready?"

"Three?"

"You, May, and the Autographic!"

THE OTHER THING Mr. Riley and I talk about is what to take pictures of: what to put in them and what to leave out. In a way, that's even more slippery than aperture and shutter. One day, though, I finally understand about how some pictures just *need* to be taken.

It's a hot July morning, and I've come awake to pots clanking in the kitchen and women talking without making any effort to be quiet. The smell of peaches being pickled, tangy and sweet and heavy, lies over everything.

In the kitchen I find Mama and Grandmama and Mrs. Mendosa well into their work.

Grandmama is at the stove dropping ripe peaches into boiling water to loosen the skins. At the same time, she stirs pickling spices into a kettle of sugar water and vinegar.

At the table Mrs. Mendosa peels and Mama cuts around the fruit, pulling juicy peach halves from pits.

Even May is busy, entertaining Mrs. Mendosa's baby. She shows him the coffee mill and the scale, the food chopper and the clothes wringer.

I'm the only one without a job. I nibble on a cold biscuit and watch, feeling rather left out. Then I get my camera.

And looking into the viewfinder, I see a picture that just needs to be taken.

I know there is not enough light to catch all the details, but that's all right. What I want is the shape of these women as I see them against the morning sun at the window.

Grandmama is standing so straight at the stove. Even when she reaches to the back of it she stands straight, her body a proud line from her shoulders to her feet.

Mama is softer lines, and graceful. She's cutting up peaches, but she could be weaving a basket or folding tea towels. I think that I want Mama to be always sitting at a table, her arms and hands still in their work, quiet.

Mrs. Mendosa, she's like Mama.

I steady the camera on a chair back and set the shutter as slow as I dare. Then I set the aperture to $f8$ and take the picture. Change it to $f6.3$. Take a third picture at $f11$.

Then I release the shutter a fourth time, to be sure.

They are three women working together, and I think I have taken a picture that tells more than just what they look like.

16

TOO SOON I BEGIN counting back from mid-September, when Nick will start college: 50 more days with him, 48, 47 ... 43 ...

I don't know why I do it; all the counting does is send a stab of regret through me that there's not some way to keep this summer from ending.

Nick's counting days, too: I know because he tells me.

Suddenly it's an August afternoon, and we're on a picnic down by the creek with May and Boy. We're done eating, and Nick's lying back, his head on my lap. He says, "If we come out here every Saturday and Sunday before I leave for school, we can come out here ten more times."

Suddenly I'm aware of May and Boy, embarrassed to see they're watching us. "Nick," I say, straightening up, "I'll take a picture."

I take three: Nick clowning, May holding up an empty cake plate, Boy smiling straight into my camera lens.

Then May spots an old stagecoach body, half buried in mesquite and brambles, and we all go to investigate, Boy leading the way.

"Watch out for snakes," May calls just as a thorny, dislodged branch whips across Boy's ankle. There are copperheads around here, and also cottonmouths and rattlers—enough poison to scare anyone, and Boy must think he's been bitten. He whirls, swatting and yelling, "Where is it? Where?"

He's so panicked that at first he doesn't even hear Nick saying, "Hey, it's a branch. You got scared by a branch."

Then Boy sees us laughing and he gets angry, ashamed of looking silly. He pushes and punches on as if every bramble is a real snake.

Mostly to soothe things, I hunt for something to take a picture of.

"Look at those," I say, pointing to initials carved in one of the coach's rotting window frames. The window is a few yards away, across a thick barrier of cactus. "Is that a '65 after the letters?"

I adjust my camera settings and cock the shutter while I look for a way to get closer.

"That cactus will cut your legs up," Nick warns. "Asia, the picture's not worth it."

"So make her a path," Boy says.

And Nick, still easygoing, answers, "I'd need an ax."

"Do without," Boy taunts, kicking at the base of the tallest bright spine. It topples, leaving a mash of pulp and needles on his boot. He kicks another piece, and this time a chunk of cactus and needles sticks in his calf.

"You're hurting yourself," May cries, and Nick says, "Boy, stop being stupid."

But Boy keeps kicking, his flailing foot making cactus fly in a dozen directions. "Can't have Asia thinking we're both afraid to make a path." Blood oozes though his pants leg, and his ankle is visibly swelling before he finally quits. "Asia, take your picture."

"No," I say. I'm frightened—something has happened here that I don't understand—and my shaking hand hits the shutter release when I'm trying to fold away the camera.

"Take your picture!" Boy yells, lunging across the smashed cactus to the window frame. He rips the whole sill loose and throws it at me. *"Take it."*

"I already did," I tell him. "By mistake, I took something."

And then Nick plunges at Boy, grabbing but only tearing a piece of his shirt. And Boy, he's pelting down the creek bed, running as if demons are after him.

I hold tight to Nick's arm. "Leave him," I say.

THAT SHOULD HAVE BEEN enough to knock sense into May. Boy scared me, and I'm not near as timid as my sister.

May, though, when we're alone in the evening, says, "Asia, we shouldn't have pushed him."

"Us!"

"Laughing because he was fooled by that stick. Asia, it's an awful burden, living up to a father who's a brave hero, the way his father is. Boy's told me."

"What does that have to do with anything?"

"Boy wouldn't want us to think he's a coward."

"And killing some cactus was supposed to prove he's not? May, Boy was...I don't know...weird out there. I do believe he was so angry that if that cactus had been on *fire* he'd have walked through it."

AGAIN BOY BLACKWELL does an about-face. When he brings the next afternoon's paper, he's smiling and nice as can be, despite how he's limping on a bandaged-up leg that must pain him every step.

By now I've already developed my film from the picnic and seen those one-after-another negatives.

There's the one I meant to take, Boy happy on our picnic, and the one I didn't. That one, the one I snapped by mistake, catches just part of Boy's face, his mouth open as if he's spewing out rage or hate. It brings back all those uneasy feelings I have about Boy, that feeling that there's something about him I know—or I remember....

For the longest time I held those negatives to the light, balancing them, Boy with the blacks and whites reversed. Which picture was the *truth* of him?

17

THE FOLLOWING WEEK Nick tells me he and Boy will be gone for a few days, off to A. & M. College to see about tests and buying cadet uniforms and getting registered for classes.

That's not fair, is my first thought. He's not supposed to go away until September.

"I'll miss you," I say.

"Hey," Nick tells me, kissing the top of my nose, "I'll come back. Will you be waiting?"

"Right here in Dust Crossing," I answer. "It's the only place I know."

BUT AT SUPPER THAT EVENING, Papa asks, "Asia, do you remember me speaking of my cousin Philip?"

"The man who writes for that magazine in Washington, D.C.?"

Papa nods. "He's in Texas working on a story at one of the army camps, and he wants to visit us while he's here. Maybe he'll look at your pictures."

Later Papa and Mama sit talking on the porch swing, thinking, I guess, that the rest of us have gone to bed.

I should tell them I'm in the living room, but theirs is such a quick conversation, coming through the open window, there's hardly time.

"You shouldn't encourage Asia over this photography business," Mama says.

From where I'm sitting I can see my parents: dark gray shapes against the black slats of the swing and the charcoal, star-dotted sky. My father takes a final draw on his pipe before knocking it out.

"Me?" he says. "You and my mother are the ones who encouraged her to start with. Paying her to do all that work so she could buy the camera. Mother even lent her some."

So he does know.

Mama, her voice wistful, says, "I'm not sure what we intended. I suppose that we just wanted Asia to have something to make her happy. Chester, what if it becomes more?"

"Such as?"

"I don't know," Mama answers. "But ... showing her work to Philip ... Washington is so far away."

Papa laughs then. "Sophie, Philip's coming *here* to Dust Crossing, and he's not likely to offer her a job!"

"But he'll tell about Washington ... about big places. Chester, I don't want to lose my daughter."

I see my father pull her to him. Their separate shapes re-form into one: Papa sitting upright with Mama's head on his shoulder.

"I suppose I'm being foolish," Mama says. "It would be harder to have a son her age just now, worrying about him having to go to war."

"The war does make everything look different," Papa says.

Whatever Mama's answer is, I can't hear it at all.

AT WORK MR. RILEY asks me to print several portraits, including some of old Mr. Mavis on his hundredth birthday.

"All by myself?"

"You're getting as good as me. And you saw that notice in the newspaper asking for whoever can spare a few hours to help with farmwork? I thought maybe instead of fishing I'd go pitch in."

He tips my grandmother a salute. "I wasn't catching anything anyway."

After he leaves I tell Grandmama I'll be in the darkroom. "You'll stay out here?" I ask.

I can't help feeling anxious whenever I leave her alone, though I haven't had any new reason to be. I never did tell my parents about that time she wandered off—partly because telling would seem disloyal and partly, I guess, because I didn't want them to stop us coming to the studio. Not telling: It makes me responsible.

"Grandmama," I repeat, "you'll watch the parlor the whole time?"

"Oh, yes."

But she crosses to the table where the appointment

book is kept and stands looking at it. "What was I...?" she murmurs. "Well, silly old woman me."

"Grandmama," I say, uneasy, "I was thinking... You've never seen how pictures are made. Would you like to watch me work?"

"In the dark?"

"I'll have on a safelight for printing. It's dim but enough to see by."

"Well, then I'd like that, Asia. A person's never too old to see something new."

PRINTING IS LIKE FILM developing in its order: using the developer, stopping its action, fixing the image, and washing off the chemicals. The difference is that printing is done in trays in the sink, and you can see every step.

I place one of Mr. Mavis's negatives on the glass surface of the printer table and then position a piece of photographic paper over it. Then I cover them with the printer's pressure pad. "Ready, Grandmama?" I ask, and press down on a foot treadle.

"Oh!" she exclaims as lamps inside the printer's light box blaze on.

I count the exposure, plunge us back into the dimness of the safelight, and slip the exposed paper into the tray of developing solution.

This is the magic.

A picture hides in the white paper that sways in a tray of developer. First you don't see anything, and then you think maybe you do but you're not sure, and then, yes, that *is* a bit of gray coming up. Quickly the image goes from nothing to sharpening black and white and every shade between.

The eyes, those are what make a photographed face real, eyes that peer up through liquid, steady and straight.

"Why, I declare," Grandmama says, "that's Mr. Mavis."

I thought maybe she would watch once or twice and then sit in the chair I've lugged in. Instead, Grandmama stays by my side while I make print after print. "Imagine," she says. "Just imagine."

And then she asks, "Asia, would it help if I move the photographs through these last trays?"

We work out a procedure, me counting exposure and handling the print in the developer, then Grandmama moving the print from the water bath to the fixer and counting the time there.

Once I hear her whisper, "Who'd ever have thought?"

We're still at it when Mr. Riley returns. "Why, Mrs. McKinna," he says, "I'm going to have to think about putting you on the payroll."

In the amber glow from the safelight, Grandmama's face lights up with pleasure.

NICK'S AT CHURCH Sunday morning, and we sit together in a back pew.

"How was A. & M.?" I whisper.

"Exciting. Swarming with students and soldiers. They are learning auto mechanics and communications, practicing infantry drills..."

96

Mama, two benches up, turns around to frown at us as Dr. Marcum, our minister, says, "Let us begin with prayers for the safety of Mary Wilson, serving with Red Cross nurses in France, and for J. B. Lancer, on board a navy ship . . ."

"Nick," I whisper, "tell me more later."

HE DOESN'T GET A CHANCE. After the service Mr. Grissom whisks him off to help with some problem at the paper, and I end up going home with my folks.

The phone's ringing when we open the door. Cousin Philip says he's almost to Dust Crossing and asks if today is convenient for getting together.

Grandmama begins pulling down the makings for biscuits. "Your mother and I will get cooking," she says. "Asia, you read us the morning paper."

May looks over my shoulder at the *Sentinel*'s front page, which has a new list of Dust Crossing boys who've volunteered for induction. This time we know almost every one.

"Look," I say, "there's Otto Schroeder. I thought he was going to college."

Mama says, "He's probably doing the thing that looks most patriotic."

"More's the pity the Schroeders think there's any need," my grandmother says. She presses her lips together. "Though I suppose as long as those fires stay unsolved, there'll be questions."

"Grandmama," I tell her, "everyone's forgotten all about those."

18

COME AFTERNOON we linger in the dining room listening to Cousin Philip tell story after story about articles he's written. He and the photographer he works with have been all over the world.

I'm trying to think how to mention my own photography when Homer does it for me.

"If you ever need somebody else to take pictures, you can hire Asia," he says. "That is, if she can't get Nick Grissom to marry her."

I kick my brother under the table, and Mama says, "Homer, behave yourself."

"Nick Grissom is Asia's beau?" Philip asks, picking up the wrong end of things.

"Sort of," I say.

Papa frowns.

"Not exactly, but..." I hurry on. "I am learning photography, working this summer as an assistant in a studio."

"My Sarah's just your age," Philip says. "She's thinking of dresses and parties all the time."

I feel a flush rising on my face. I'm not sure if I've been criticized or not.

But then he adds, "I'd like to see some of your photos."

HE DOESN'T MENTION it again, but later, when I'm helping with the cleanup, pouring water into a dishpan, Grandmama says, "Leave that, Asia. Go show your pictures to your cousin."

And Mama, despite that talk I overheard, nods. "Go ahead."

So I take the half dozen photographs that I think are my very best to the front porch.

Philip spreads them on the railing: the two that show trees against skies full of puffy clouds; the one I took the morning we canned pickled peaches; May playing her guitar; a shot of half of Dust Crossing's population watching a troop train pull in.

He studies them a long while. "You use a tripod?"

I shake my head.

"You should."

Philip shuffles the photographs; comes back, finally, to the one of Mama and Grandmama and Mrs. Mendosa working in the kitchen. "Why did you take this, Asia?"

I think back, trying to come up with an answer that makes sense.

"It was their shapes," I say finally. "I wanted to

remember how they were. Because . . . how different each shape was . . . it said something about who the women were."

I stop, feeling like a fool, but Philip is nodding.

"I think we can use it," he says. "We pay three dollars for onetime rights."

I think my mouth drops open. I *know* my father's does, at least for an instant. "You want to *buy* Asia's photograph?" he asks. "And put it in your magazine? Philip, you don't need to do that."

"I'll use it with the story I'm thinking about on Texas life," Philip answers.

He turns back to me. "Well, Asia?"

I swallow hard. "Please, what are onetime rights?"

And then he starts laughing, and Papa laughs with him, their laughter ringing out.

"It means you'll sell us the right to publish your photograph but that it will still belong to you." Cousin Philip hands the pictures back. "Nice work, Asia."

He sucks on his pipe. "So, Chester, tell me about this fishing trip you're planning."

I'M PASSING BY THE PORCH window when I hear Papa ask, "Philip, I suppose this camera interest is just a passing fancy with Asia, but if it's not . . . what would you advise?"

What is Papa asking?

I wait, hardly breathing, for Philip's answer. "After high school? Well, you might send her where she can be part of all the change that's coming—not just in equipment, but in what can be *done* with cameras. The war's shown all kinds of new uses—photos for news, aerial photography..."

"Whoa," Papa says. "Let's at least keep Asia on the ground."

Philip laughs. "I do get carried away. But she ought to go where she can become familiar with the best work that's being done. Choose a college in some city where she can join a camera club. Perhaps work in a good studio. New York, Chicago, maybe."

"So far away!" Papa says.

My thoughts echo what I've heard... college, camera club, New York... *NEW YORK!*

Suddenly time seems to both stretch out and fold in. I see myself, grown-up, on a city street with buildings and countless automobiles, surrounded by people I don't know. I see myself, and my stomach quakes, I am so scared. I almost run out to the porch to say, I don't want to go, Papa. I just want to take pictures of my family.

I almost go out on the porch and tell him, except, just then, I hear Grandmama walking down the hall and Mama following quickly after her.

"Ella," Mama is saying, "you misunderstood. I was trying to say anyone can forget to put in baking powder."

But Grandmama has shut her bedroom door, and after a moment Mama goes back to the kitchen. It is the first I realize we didn't have any biscuits with dinner.

———

THE BAD THING ABOUT the pictures you have only in your mind is that sometimes they are just *imagined* sights to go with sounds you don't want to hear. I know I will never, as long as I live, forget walking by my grandmother's door and hearing her quiet crying.

19

THE FISHING TRIP: It's the single most wonderful thing that is planned for all this summer and is the one part of summer that hasn't changed as long as I can remember. Every year my family and the Grissoms load up camping gear and food and head somewhere.

When I tell Mr. Riley about it, he says, "Asia, I don't know how I'll get along without your help." Then he hands me a half dozen rolls of film. "Now, you take pictures of everything."

Mrs. Grissom and Mama talk on the telephone several times each day. "Nell, you're bringing preserves?" Mama asks. "I'll do the vegetables. Do you think five batches of corn bread will be enough?"

And then, a few days before we're to leave, Mrs. Grissom shows up at the back door with a list of cooking utensils. "Give this to your mama, Asia," she tells me. "I've marked what I'll pack."

She pauses to run a finger under the collar of her

dress, which, despite the heat, she's got buttoned clear up to her neck.

Then she adds, "Oh, and tell her we won't need quite so much food. Nick won't be going."

Nick not...! "Why not?"

"Because the *Sentinel* press keeps breaking down, and as long as this war's on, Mr. Grissom can't get new parts to fix it properly. He wants to stay himself to keep it running, but I told him that would spoil the trip for everyone."

"Why can't Boy stay?"

"Boy doesn't know how the press works." Mrs. Grissom's face softens just a little. "Asia, I'm sorry."

It's not fair. It's really not fair.

IT'S NOT FAIR, I'm thinking, as I place a negative on the printer glass. The camping trip was going to be the last big thing Nick and I did together this summer, and now he's not going.

I'm printing yet another picture of a young man in a stiff new uniform. I expose the photographic paper and move it into developer.

Grandmama's at my elbow watching the image come up. "Poor thing," she says. "Just look how frightened he is."

"He should be," I answer, thinking of the bad news that's come to Dust Crossing in recent days: The last two War Department casualty lists had the names of local men on them. One was J. B. Lancer, who ought to be starting his senior year with me.

"Although," I continue, as I watch the darkening grays and blacks of the picture in front of me, "this soldier seems more angry than anything."

"Look at his eyes, Asia," Grandmama says. "The poor boy is frightened."

The corners do wrinkle in a rigid squint. *Anger or fright, one or the other.*

But, I realize, I've seen just that squint somewhere else.

On Boy Blackwell, when he destroyed the cactus.

I TAKE ONE MORE PHOTOGRAPH before we leave for our camping trip.

It's the afternoon before we're to go. Grandmama has called me into her room and put some coins in my hand. "There, Asia," she says, "you run those down to the newspaper office. This will finish the Thrift Cards, and you can turn them in for five-dollar War Savings Stamps."

"Now?"

"And if you run into Nick, you invite him for dinner. Tell him you made a lemon pie."

"I only squeezed the lemon juice. You did all the rest."

"Asia, you don't have to tell everything you know."

"Grandmama..."

"Go on now."

My grandmama. She loves me so much.

On impulse I ask, "Grandmama, before I leave...I have a roll of film I'd like to finish up. Can I get my camera and take your photograph?"

"Why, certainly, though I don't know why you want a picture of an old woman."

We go out front for the outside light. Looking at the three sections of the range finder, I adjust the Autographic's focus until the image in them is an unbroken line.

"Wait, Asia," Grandmama says. She rubs her cheeks to bring color to them and bites her lips to make them darker. "Now," she says, setting her mouth in the half smile she saves for photographs.

GRANDMAMA MUST BE LISTENING for me to get back from the *Sentinel* office, because as soon as I come in she calls me to her room.

"Asia," she asks, "did I ever show you how I looked when I was young?"

"I'd like to see again."

Grandmama hands me a photograph from a box. It's one I've seen a hundred times before: Grandmama when she was about my age. In it she wears a high-collared dress edged in lace, and her hair is fixed in a low bun.

"All of us Allison girls were known for having sweet smiles," she says. Then, talking more to herself than to me, she adds, "I was pretty in my time, wasn't I?"

Grandmama abruptly takes the picture back.

"Asia," she says, "I want you to promise me that when your children ask what their great-grandmother looked like, you'll show them that picture of me young rather than some photograph of an old woman."

"I promise, Grandmama," I say, laughing a bit.

"Asia, I don't *feel* the way I look."

DINNER'S OVER —"the best lemon pie I ever ate," Nick said—and Nick and I are out back at One-Eye's pen.

I've been telling him how I feel about his not going on our trip.

"Asia," he says, "I feel the same way, but I can't help what I have to do." He holds out a scrap of lettuce to my tortoise. "Besides, staying here, I can come look in on this guy every day."

"I'd rather One-Eye be lonely than me. Nick, camping won't be any fun without you."

A red-gold shaft of light from the setting sun moves across the wall of the chicken house, and a window flashes with its flame. I guess it reminds us both of the same thing.

"Did you ever learn anything about who burned the old coop?" Nick asks.

"Nothing," I answer. "Papa supposes we never will."

20

MAMA IS UP, even though the house is still dark. I hear her working in the kitchen; hear the crackle and sputter of food being put into hot fat.

The air smells of cooking chicken. Mama must be frying it for us to eat cold for lunch along the way.

I imagine her standing at the stove, turning flour-coated drumsticks in melted lard, letting them sizzle until they're golden. Then she'll put a lid on the heavy black skillet and let them continue to cook.

I lie still, enjoying the feel of the early morning air, enjoying the last moments of doing nothing but also thinking about Mama downstairs.

A saying I've heard Papa quote more than once comes to me: "Man may work from sun to sun, but woman's work is never done."

Get up, Asia, I tell myself. *Get up, wake May, and go help.*

NICK COMES TO SEE US off and to give a hand loading the automobiles.

Picnic hampers and clothes and fishing gear go wherever they'll fit. Papa checks and double-checks that all his emergency tools are packed. Mr. Grissom worries over where to put the extra cans of gasoline.

Our big canvas tent is strapped on the raised top of Papa's Model T, along with a rolled-up shade tarp. Heavier things like the huge cooking kettle go on the Grissoms' Dodge sedan.

After May and Boy and I choose the backseat of the Grissoms' automobile—Grandmama and Homer will ride in the backseat of ours—the door on the passenger side gets closed and then sleeping cots are hung along the outside.

"Asia," Nick says at the window, "set your camera and hand it through, and I'll take a picture of all this."

But I can see from the way he aims the Autographic that I'm the one he's photographing. "And now I'll take a picture of you," I tell him.

Then Homer darts in front of Nick.

> *Nick loves Asia.*
> *How will he get along?*
> *All alone*
> *When Asia's gone?*

"Homer!" I fuss, shaking my head to show Nick I am helpless to do a thing about my brother.

"Maybe his poetry is improving," Nick suggests.

109

MIDMORNING: The drive is hot and getting hotter. We are all dreading the afternoon.

NOONTIME: We stop for lunch. The chicken is about the best Mama has ever made. When we start driving again, we're on a dirt road that angles southwest.

MIDAFTERNOON: If we close ourselves in, we suffocate from heat. If we don't, we suffocate in clouds of dust. The dry land stretches to broken bluffs in the distance now.

"I can't tell one part of this country from another," May says.

"Just Texas," Boy answers her.

But everywhere I look I see a different scene: mesquite and broken rocks one way, bands of sheep or goats another. The low hills ahead shade from gray-orange to hazy purple.

Finally we cross the Pecos River and follow its western side down to where a clear creek empties into it. It's a place where the rough canyon is softened by large trees and grass.

It's a pretty spot for camping, and I wish Nick were here to see it.

WE QUICKLY SETTLE INTO the easy ways of camp life. The Grissoms' friends join us, and that makes us eleven in all, though just four of us kids: Homer, May and me, and Boy.

Though I expected Boy to be hanging around May all the time, we hardly see him. Mostly he spends his time fishing with the men and hanging around them in the evening. "Trying to prove he's grown-up," I tell May.

"Don't be so mean, Asia," she says. But I know she's a little hurt that he's not paying her more attention.

Anyway, May and Homer and I are pretty much left to do as we please. Besides, of course, doing chores.

"Asia," May asks, "why are you taking a picture of me scrubbing a skillet?"

"Because I promised Mr. Riley."

Also, taking pictures helps keep me from missing Nick.

I intend to shoot all six rolls.

"Well, just don't follow me when I go off to pee," May says.

21

DUST CROSSING RULES don't apply on the Pecos.

Homer gets away with eating whatever he wants whenever he wants, and nobody says, "Homer, don't spoil your appetite."

Mama lazes with novels for long hours at a time, often lying in a huge old live oak tree at the place where one of · its heavy limbs touches the ground and then grows up again.

Papa and Mr. Grissom, who don't approve of betting, lay a two-bit wager on who can catch the biggest catfish. Mr. Grissom pays a quarter after Papa lands one that feeds us all, with leftovers.

And I *think* Mrs. Grissom leaves off her petticoat.

PHPPTT, PHPPTT. Homer is seeing how far he can spit watermelon seeds.

A wet seed lands on my leg, and the next hits May on her forehead.

"What do you think?" I ask May.

"I think we can catch him if we want."

We chase him around the camp until sweat streams down my face.

"I may die," I call to May.

"Me, too."

Then Homer, red-faced and panting, runs too close to where Mama is resting. He comes up against her outstretched arm the way he might run into a fence he hasn't seen.

Mama helps us drag him down the path to the river and throw him in.

"It's not fair," Homer bellows. "There's three of you."

"Sophie," Papa calls, "you're scaring the fish."

"Sorry! Girls," Mama says, "we must be still."

And with that she drops into the shallow, slow current, clothes and all, and after a moment May and I do, too.

The sun pounds down, and the river water is bathwarm. Papa and the other men shake their heads. Boy stares at May, or maybe at the way she looks coming out of the water, and she smiles back.

"May," I whisper, "he's ignored you for days. Have some pride."

GRANDMAMA DOESN'T WORRY ABOUT our sopping clothes when we walk into camp. "They'll dry," she says. "In this heat they'll dry in no time."

But she does worry about our uncovered heads.

"In my day girls wouldn't have thought of going out in the sun without hats. You'll ruin your complexions."

She's wearing her bonnet, a thing she says is ages old but just what a camping trip calls for.

"If you're not careful," she scolds, "the sun will make your minds weak."

"Asia and May already have weak minds," Homer says.

"Homer," Mama asks, "haven't you learned your lesson?"

EACH EVENING we set supper out on a long makeshift table. There are platters of all kinds of food, the biggest platters heaped with fish. Relish, tomatoes, apricots, and pickled beets shine green and red-orange and purple among the tawny colors of baking and frying.

After supper the men stand apart, smoking their pipes and joking. I watch my father and the others, notice how they slouch, elbows swinging out and hands resting on their hips. Men, I think, take up more space than women do, and it's not just because they're bigger.

Boy, too.

"Don't stare, Asia," Mama says. "It's not polite."

I get my camera instead.

AND SUDDENLY IT'S OUR LAST full day of camping.

The grown-ups decide on some sight-seeing. Mrs. Grissom wants to look for a pictograph cave, and Papa and the other men say they'd like to explore the remains of old Fort Lancaster if they can get to the east side of the river.

"You all go on," Grandmama tells the others. "I'll stay here with the children."

Mama thanks her, but a little later on it's me she asks, "Asia, you'll keep an eye on Homer?"

"As much as he'll let me."

"And watch your grandmother, Asia." Mama glances over to where Grandmama is putting away the breakfast things. "She seems to ... these days ... I'm not sure ..."

"I know, Mama," I say.

Then the six of them are piling into the Grissom automobile, Mr. Grissom urging, "Crowd in, crowd in, we'll all fit."

Mrs. Grissom leans out the window toward Boy. "We'll count on you to be the man here today," she says. "You take care of the others, Boy."

"I will," he answers.

I wonder if I'm the only one who sees the look he flashes May, and her surprise, and then the nod she sends back.

22

WE WAVE TO THE AUTOMOBILE as it sets off. All at once our camp seems very lonely, just canvas and five people.

Boy picks up a fishing pole.

"Can I come?" Homer asks.

"No."

And May, after starting to protest, "You're going fishing? But I thought...," seems to remember her pride. "Asia," she says, "I think I'll read magazines."

"I'm going to take a few last pictures," I tell her, "and then I'll read, too."

"What about me?" Homer says.

"Did you find those fifty different insects you were after," Grandmama asks him, "or do you want me to point out a few?"

IN EARLY AFTERNOON the temperature reaches its most sweltering yet, and not a breath of breeze moves under the rolled-up sides of the tent, where May and Grandmama and I are stretched out on cots.

Homer is over near the food table, busy building something with sticks and pebbles.

I listen to Grandmama's breath become a soft sputter of sleep. Then I close my eyes and try to slow my own breathing; I wish I could sleep past the day's heat.

"May!" Boy's voice is a whisper. "May!"

She gets up, and I ask, "Where are you going?"

"Just to talk to Boy. Maybe we'll take a walk."

"Stay close."

"Asia, you're not Mama."

MAY WON'T GO FAR, I tell myself.

Still, as the minutes drag on I wonder if I shouldn't have invited myself along on their walk. *And probably been turned down as fast as Boy said no to Homer going fishing.*

Half an hour. Forty-five minutes.

I slip off the cot, and get my camera so I'll have some excuse to poke about. Homer's intent on his work and doesn't even hear me come up. "Did you notice which way May and Boy went?" I ask.

"When?"

Annoyed with my sister at first—this is too hot an afternoon to have to go hunting for her—and then increasingly concerned, I search in a widening circle.

She and Boy are not in the camp. Not at the river, either, not so that I can see anyway. Maybe, I think, I'll go back and honk the car horn. They'll answer that.

But just then I hear a scuffle and what sounds like a slap and then Boy's threatening, hoarse order: "Shut up."

"May?"

There's a cutoff whine and then silence.

"May?" I call, louder, running now toward the rock outcropping where the sounds came from.

And then May appears from behind the rocks, stepping along the river's gravel edge. Her body is an unbending line of dignity, but her face is flaming red and splotched with the imprint of a hand.

"May?"

"Walk, Asia," she says, stepping past me. "Just come on!"

"I HATE HIM," May says as we go back to camp. "I hate him! I hate him!"

"May, what did he do?"

"Oh, Asia, nothing really, but . . . he was getting fresh. I mean, not exactly . . . but I raised my hand pretending to slap him. I thought we were *playing*. Only, Asia, he grabbed it and . . ." May's face flames deeper scarlet. "Asia, he slapped *me*."

"Papa will take a whip to him."

May turns frantic at that idea. "Asia, don't tell. Promise. For people to know Boy hit me . . . Asia, I'd be mortified."

GRANDMAMA IS STILL ASLEEP when we reach camp, but Homer's migrated from the food table to Papa's automobile.

"May," I argue, "you're going to have to explain *something*. For one thing, your cheekbone's going to bruise."

Suddenly noise comes from where Homer is, the

sound of him cranking the automobile and the engine starting. *What?*

Before I can holler at him, May says, "Don't wake Grandmama. I don't want her to see me."

So I have to run clear over to my brother, who's now inside the car, behind the steering wheel.

"Homer," I tell him, "out, now!"

"Let me go just across camp and back. Papa lets me drive with him. I know how."

"Now!"

But just then Boy comes into sight. "May," he calls, "I'm sorry."

May flings open the car's passenger-side door. "Come on, Asia."

"Are you crazy?"

"Let's scare him. Make him *think* we're going after Papa. Homer, drive."

Homer, confused, mumbles, "What?"

Boy is almost up to us now, and I can see clearly his smile—that same miserably contrite, *phony* smile I've seen before. It makes me want to get even with him.... Make him feel as foolish and mortified as he made May feel. And scared.

"Homer," I say, scrambling in, "we're going to play a trick on Boy. Let's go!"

And when Homer doesn't move, I yell at him, "Hurry! We want to leave Boy behind."

The car starts rolling just as Boy reaches us, his face showing every emotion I'd hoped would be there.

"Hey!" he yells. "Wait!"

I open my camera and line him up in the viewfinder, past the rear of the car, Boy just *left,* looking foolish.

"Maybe that's the truth of Boy," I say as I release the shutter. "He's a fool."

I know the picture won't come out, not taken from a moving automobile and without a single camera setting right, but Boy won't know. He'll dread the picture I took.

We're getting away from camp now, and Homer starts to pull around the steering wheel to turn us back.

"No," I tell him. "A little more. Let's go just five or ten minutes."

"You mean it?" Homer asks.

"Yes," May answers. "Drive."

A sudden thought worries me. "Grandmama," I say. "I promised to watch Grandmama."

"She's sleeping," May says. "Homer, faster!"

I'm the oldest. I should stop us, but I don't. I just don't.

The beaten path we're following twists past trees, quickly taking us out of sight of the tents, beyond Boy's voice calling us to return.

"Now where?" shouts Homer.

I should say, "Back to camp." With all the noise, my grandmother must be awake. She'll be worried, I know, but still I don't give the order to turn around.

And May is urging Homer to keep going.

Homer and May, it's like they've taken leave of their senses.

And me, too. As we climb up out of the trees, all I caution is, "Don't get us lost."

Homer jerks a thumb over his shoulder so I'll see the dusty trail we're putting down, the tire prints and smashed plants.

We speed up even more, and suddenly I feel like we're Robinson Crusoe and the Swiss Family Robinson and every adventurer I've ever read about, adventurers staring across oceans and into unknown wilderness. It is... wonderful.

Then, "Be careful," May cries out, and the automobile jolts to a stop that throws us all forward. A stop that leaves the car tilting way down at the front corner on Homer's side.

"What happened?" I ask, but Homer is already out his door and investigating. White splotches appear through the sunburn on his face.

"No. Oh, no." He barely breathes the words.

"Homer!"

"Asia"—Homer's voice is panicking—"the wheel is wedged between two rocks," and the size of his panic tells me we are not going to be able to pull it out.

"Papa's going to kill me," he says.

"Asia?" May asks.

And I am Asia again, the oldest, and in charge and responsible, and I don't feel like Robinson Crusoe at all. I get out and look at the wheel, buried to its hub between the sheared halves of a broken boulder.

"I guess we better start walking," I say.

23

WE WALK, IT SEEMS, a long time, but the men in Mr. Grissom's car reach us before the tents have even come in sight.

Papa is so angry he won't speak, and I end up explaining about the wheel to Mr. Grissom. "We figured it would be something like that," he says. "Get in."

We drive back to the stuck auto, following along the tracks in the red dust. "Papa," I say once, "I'm sorry."

He doesn't answer.

After the men have put a tow chain on our car and jerked it out though, after they've jacked it up and changed the tire, Papa suddenly turns to me. "You like to have killed your grandmother."

MAMA IS IN THE TENT putting wet rags on Grandmama's feverish arms and legs: slack skin over fragile bone.

"May I help?" I ask. "Please?"

While May cries I help Mama re-wet the skin-heated

cloths in water that is only as cool as the river is warm.

Once Boy comes up to May. I hear him say, "I didn't see her walk off; I didn't know she was gone."

May turns her back.

I don't cry until Mama changes the cloth on Grandmama's face and I see how red the skin is, how Grandmama's eyes are swollen shut. Grandmama, who always says, "Wear your hat; take care of your complexion; men don't like women to look like farmhands."

"She went after you without even her bonnet," Mama says.

"Grandmama," I whisper. "Oh, Grandmama, I'm sorry."

A while later Grandmama says in a voice so low I can hardly hear, "Asia, honey, thank you for coming for me, child. I knew, when I was wandering in all that heat, you'd come get me."

"But you were coming for us..."

"Now, child," she says, "your grandmother understands more than you think."

A FEW DAYS AFTERWARD we drive to Dust Crossing, a journey that starts before dawn from the tiny sanitarium where Grandmama has gotten care, a journey that lasts into evening. It is a hard trip for her, but she won't be talked into breaking it into two days. She insists we are all ready to be home.

And the next morning, when May and I say we're

going to take turns caring for her until she's up and out of bed, she says, "You will not. Two young people cooped up with an old woman? Fiddlesticks."

GRANDMAMA GETS BETTER much faster than anyone expects her to. It seems no time from when she says, "I believe I will eat with the family tonight," to when she announces, "Asia and May, our garden needs attention."

Gradually the shame and guilt I feel about causing my grandmother to be hurt lessens. It's partly, I guess, because once school starts up I have things like lessons that take my attention, and partly because nobody else seems interested.

Grandmama won't admit I have anything to apologize for, and Mama and Papa don't punish May and Homer and me. There's no need, Mama says.

Even Nick listens just so long. Then he says, "Asia, I get the idea."

Five minutes more and he's asking me to promise to go to the first college dance with him, and, of course, that's when Homer shows up.

Nick and Asia
Kiss, kiss, kiss.

Nick interrupts with his own finish, looking straight into my eyes:

Nick tells Asia,
I'll miss, miss, miss
You.

"Nick," I tell him, "that is really bad."
"I know," he says. "Let's go back to the *kiss* part."
Homer yells, "Dis*gust*ing."

24

STILL, NO MATTER HOW forgiving everybody is, I can't bring myself to develop any of the camping trip film. I don't ever want to see its last-picture reminder of that car ride and its results.

And if I don't want reminding of that, May doesn't want reminding of that or Boy, either. She's made me promise not to tell a soul about how he behaved. It worried me until I realized he's making a point of staying away from us. Another kid is delivering papers on our street now, and soon Boy will be off at school anyway.

As will Nick.

I can't believe how fast our last days together go by. Suddenly it's a Saturday morning in mid-September, and in another six hours he'll catch a train for College Station.

I'm in the kitchen arguing with Grandmama.

"Asia," she tells me, "you can't go empty-handed to see your young man off to school."

"I don't make very good cakes, Grandmama."

"You'll make this one good."

She stands over me while I beat the eleven egg yolks of a ladyfinger recipe.

"Harder, Asia. I want to see *blisters* atop that batter."

I SHOW HER THE lace-trimmed yellow dress I've put on to wear to the depot. "Do I look all right?"

"Pretty as can be." Grandmama hands me a small, single strand of pearls. "Here, Asia," she says, "put these on. And use my hand mirror to see yourself from the back."

AND THEN NICK'S climbing into the coach, calling last good-byes to his folks and me. "Remember, Asia," he shouts, "you're coming over for the first dance."

Boy's already gotten on board, disappearing without saying good-bye to anyone in particular, not even his aunt and uncle.

A WEEK OR SO LATER, Papa brings home a letter from Cousin Philip. Inside there's a three-dollar check made out to Miss Asia McKinna.

I can't do much but grin. I'm going to finish paying for my camera with money I *earned* from a *picture*!

"What does he say?" Mama asks.

Papa, reluctantly, I think, reads aloud, " 'I've talked with my wife about Asia's interest in photography, and we'd like to invite her to visit around Thanksgiving. We'll be taking our Sarah to look at colleges then, and Asia would be welcome to come along. We could take in some museums and perhaps a photographic studio or two in Philadelphia and New York.' "

Philadelphia. *New York...!* "Oh, Papa," I exclaim. "May I go? Please?"

My father shakes his head. "Asia, we can't afford such a trip. Or an East Coast college, for that matter."

"But..."

"Even train tickets are expensive, Asia."

Grandmama reaches out to pat my arm. "Maybe something will turn up, child," she says.

I can't imagine what, but somehow just being invited sets me dreaming and taking more pictures than ever.

GRANDMAMA AND I are going down to the studio after school two or three afternoons a week now. With Nick gone it's my favorite time, whether I'm doing jobs for Mr. Riley or working with my own pictures.

I still mess up a lot of shots, but I'm taking some that look pretty good. And finally I get around to developing the film with that picture of Grandmama I took the afternoon before we left on our camping trip.

I know as soon as I hold the negative to the light that I've got the picture I wanted.

Now I put into it every printing skill that Mr. Riley has taught me: I cut a piece of photographic paper into narrow strips to test for exposure time. Then, after I've picked the best overall time, I still regulate the lights in the printer table to give the least exposure where my negative is thin and to give the most where I want my print to be dark.

When I carry out the finished portrait, wet and cradled on a towel, the others look at it for long seconds. The picture shows the soft webbing of skin over the delicate bones of Grandmama's face and neck; her keen, washed-out eyes; and—somehow—the kindness and strength under it all.

Mr. Riley clears his throat. "Asia, this is the best picture you have ever taken."

"My," Grandmama says, "is this how I look?"

MY GRANDMAMA IS QUIET on the walk home, but as we near our house she says, "Asia, I don't want you to forget your promise. When your children ask what I looked like, you show them a picture from when I was young."

"Grandmama," I say, "you can show them yourself."

"Asia, you remember."

25

WHAT, I WONDER, is my grandmother remembering the afternoon I come on her standing at our back fence, again gazing across Mr. Lockett's field, where his kids are harvesting a last few rows of cotton?

"Want to help me get some squash, Grandmama?" I call.

She doesn't answer, just keeps staring at the patchy crop of plants stunted by the long dryness of the past summer.

"With cotton it's always something," Grandmama says. "With cotton it's always something."

I get busy searching through running squash vines and hardly notice Grandmama walk back to the house.

When I see her again, she's on her way into the new chicken coop with the kerosene can in her hand. *What?*

I go running after her.

"Grandmama," I say, pushing open the door.

She stands at a nesting ledge gathering straw into a

neat pile. Two angry hens peck at her hands. "Shoo," she's telling them. "Let me tidy up enough that I've got a place to work."

"What are you doing, Grandmama?" I ask.

"Fixing to fill the lanterns to trap boll weevils," Grandmama says. "They'll fly to the light and burn up."

I wrap my arms around my middle, then unwrap them so that I can hold her. *So it was my grandmother I glimpsed under the pecan tree, a shape tinier, after all, than I'd thought; my grandmother had started the fire.* "Let's go to the house, Grandmama," I say. "I'll finish that later."

"Well... if you're sure..."

It's not until we're on the porch that Grandmama's firm steps falter. She turns and looks back at the chicken house, then at the kerosene can I'm carrying.

"Oh," she says. "Oh, no."

THAT EVENING MAMA, PAPA, May, Homer, and I hold a family conference after Grandmama's gone to her room.

I've told them about the kerosene. Papa was shocked, Mama saddened but not very surprised.

"What are we going to do?" I ask.

"Not much different," Papa says, rubbing his neck. "Except we'll have to be extra careful not to leave your grandmother alone."

"I mean... how do we make her better?"

"I don't think there is a way, Asia," Mama answers. "This is just what happens sometimes."

Homer says, "It's already happening to Asia, gone batty over Nick and—"

Even as Mama starts to reprimand him, Homer's straining voice cracks.

A few minutes later he goes down the hall, and I hear him stop at Grandmama's room. "Are you awake, Grandmama?" he asks. "Would you like to play dominoes?"

Papa, still rubbing his neck, says, "Those lantern traps—they never did work on boll weevils anyway."

And Mama—I do believe Mama intends to read aloud the entire *Sentinel* before going to bed. Maybe it's her way of not thinking.

She reads the war news—an armistice about to be signed with Bulgaria and hope for a peace offer from Turkey—and the weather report and the personal items, her voice hardly changing.

She cuts out a request from the Federal Food Administrator that people save nutshells and fruit pits. They're needed to make carbon for masks to protect our soldiers from the German poison gas.

She goes over a story about the Spanish influenza that's spreading from up North, killing thousands in cities and on military bases alike. "Those poor people," Mama says. "Those poor people."

BY EARLY OCTOBER the influenza has reached Dust Crossing, though the *Sentinel* is not outright admitting it. Mr. Grissom first prints just a very small story that says while no one should be alarmed by local illness, all should practice good hygiene and take sensible precautions.

The next morning, though, Dust Crossing schools close because attendance is so low, and in the afternoon Mrs. Grissom telephones to say Boy and Nick are on their way home from college. "That flu is sweeping through dormitories," she says, "and they've both caught it."

It's a strange kind of sickness, one that seems to hit healthy adults as hard as it hits the babies and old people you'd expect to be most in danger. Soon every *Sentinel* carries news of another death, or two or three: a mother who leaves young children; a farmer just twenty-five years old.

Mama's so afraid of germs she won't let me go see Nick even after he and Boy are on their way to getting well, and she worries about Papa going to the depot every day.

It's Grandmama, though, who, one mid-October afternoon, turns from her baking to say, "I believe I need to sit down."

By dinner her walk is unsteady, and Mama is trying to convince her to go to bed, when suddenly Grandmama's legs buckle and she falls.

"Chester!" Mama calls. *"Chester!"*

Half an hour later my parents and I are standing with Dr. Craven on the front porch. "I hope I'm soon done seeing new cases," he says.

"But she's going to be all right?" Mama asks.

"That depends on whether the influenza goes into

pneumonia." Dr. Craven bends down for the newspaper. "I think this war is bound to end soon."

GRANDMAMA'S BEDROOM becomes the center of the house, and nothing beyond it feels real. School is still closed anyway, and even Nick's being in Dust Crossing seems like something that doesn't concern me.

Mama and May and I take turns nursing Grandmama, all of us wearing gauze masks to keep from getting sick ourselves.

We see she has the hot tea, cold compresses, and fresh air that Dr. Craven ordered. And we do the things he didn't talk about: bringing her the bedpan and changing her nightgown, sponging her arms and legs and washing soiled sheets.

Once, when Grandmama is having a good moment, she whispers, "Asia, this is no work for a young girl."

Mostly, though, Grandmama doesn't have good moments, and I think we all know in our hearts that she will die. It makes listening to her so important. I try to catch everything she says and wish I'd listened better, talked with her more, before.

Now what she says seems to be pulled up from a place inside her where occasions fifty years apart happen one right after another.

"Here, Bertha," she tells me once, when I've put a cool cloth on her forehead, "go warm yourself at the stove. And you get your lessons."

"I'm Asia," I say, but Grandmama doesn't hear.

Another time she cries out, "Don't scold that child."

And still another, "I had beaux, too. 'You may kiss me on my cheek,' I told my beaux..."

"...married in my mother's parlor..."

"...don't tell me my husband is dying..."

One afternoon tears trickle down her face as she whispers, "There's more I want to do, things I want to do over."

"What, Grandmama?" I ask, leaning close and hearing her struggle to breathe.

I try to make out her words, make sense of snatches of sentences about fishing trips and about how food tastes so good when you eat it outside.

Then her whisper turns frantic. "But what did we put it on? Bertha? Where did we put the food?"

"On tables, Grandmama. Don't you remember the long camp tables?"

But she's slipped into a fretful sleep.

SCHOOL REOPENS the fourth week of October, but instead of going I take film down to Mr. Riley's. "I need these for my grandmother," I tell him, and he doesn't question me further.

I PULL A CHAIR UP to Grandmama's bed. "I've brought camping pictures for you to look at. See us all at supper? How the food is all laid out on the table?"

Grandmama's shaky hand holds the photograph close as she studies it. "Mr. McKinna always did like a fish fry," she says. "I can hear him now, how he'd call, 'Ella, we about ready to eat?'"

I'm going to show her other pictures, but her hand drops to her chest and she shuts her eyes. Just when I think she's gone to sleep I hear her say, "Thank you, child."

GRANDMAMA PASSES AWAY two evenings later, dying so quietly that no one knows just when.

Mama sits up until dawn sewing a burying dress of taffeta silk. Papa tries to get her to go to bed, but I hear her answer, "I'd rather be doing something."

ALL THE DAY I keep turning around, feeling that if I turn fast enough I'll see Grandmama ready to talk to me; hear her say, I'm still here, child; have her help me make sense of her not being.

Then, the following morning, the morning she's to be buried, I wake to air that seems impossibly empty. I hear May and Mama down in the kitchen, Papa out back with Homer.

Grandmama, I'm not ready for you to be gone. Please look over my shoulder.

I spread pictures on my bed, the one of food on the long camp table and all the others, the pictures I won't ever get to show Grandmama now.

There's Papa with his fishing pole and a string of fish.

Mama, Mrs. Grissom, and Homer side-by-side, biting into huge wedges of watermelon.

An underexposed shot of Boy standing in the shade of a mesquite, a hunched, dark shape framed by tree limbs... *I've seen that picture before.* When I printed it, of course, but also... before that...

But I must be wrong, I think. Boy never camped with us before.

It's in the way he's standing, his shape beneath that tree limb. I saw that....

I know when. I saw that shape under the pecan tree the night our chicken house burned.

But...

"Asia," Mama calls, "come to breakfast."

26

I THOUGHT MAYBE just the Grissoms would come to hear Dr. Marcum's prayers for Grandmama. Mr. Riley is one of the first to arrive at the church, though, and behind him is Mrs. Mendosa and her husband, and behind them are more people than I had any idea Grandmama knew.

The Grissoms have Nick and Boy with them, all four looking strained. Mrs. Grissom's been crying, and Boy looks more sullen than I've ever seen him. And when Mr. Schroeder and Otto, who's in Dust Crossing on his first leave, come into the sanctuary, Nick actually holds Boy in place.

"Boy's father died this morning of the influenza," I hear Mr. Grissom whisper to Mama. "We received a telegram from the naval hospital."

And the Germans killed his father by putting him there, Boy's thinking, sure as if Mr. Blackwell died of bullets.

WE'RE AT THE CEMETERY, our minister saying final words over Grandmama's grave, when I see Boy slip away. Suddenly I have to talk to him *now*. I have to *ask* him those questions that have filtered every prayer and every word I've heard this morning.

"Asia?" Nick asks as I start after Boy. "Are you going back to your house? May I walk with you?"

"No," I tell him. "That is . . . there's something I have to work out myself."

I hasten between rows of headstones and out the cemetery gate. By now Boy's down the road almost to where town starts. He disappears around a corner, and I begin running.

He's gone to the right somewhere, across the Farm-to-Market Road, toward the cotton gin and stockyards. I hurry past milling cattle being herded into a chute; dodge between the wagons and automobiles of farm families on Saturday errands; and have to wait for a train to go by.

Then suddenly I'm beyond the confusion of noise and bustle, in side streets and alleys. *Where did he go?*

I pass the wool co-op and cut across a field, and finally I spot Boy hurrying by the long, board fence of Schroeder Lumber.

"Boy!" I shout. "Wait up."

"Asia, go home."

"No. I've got to ask you something."

He waits just long enough for me to reach him. "Go home," he says again.

"Boy . . . the night our chicken house burned, you were there, weren't you? When the fire started, I mean?"

"You're crazy." He shakes my hand off his arm and starts away.

"I'm not crazy. I can see the picture."

I'm talking, of course, about the picture in my mind,

but Boy doesn't know that. He's suddenly in front of me. "What picture? Where?"

"Of you around back of my house. That is, I didn't know it was you . . . and I thought my grandmother started the fire . . . Boy, did you? Did you burn the chicken house?"

"No." But Boy's eyes shift from mine in that flicking, off-center gaze. . . . *He's lying.* . . . "Where's the photo? I want it."

"So it *was* you I saw under the pecan tree!"

What if I let Grandmama believe she started that fire when she didn't? . . . Because I didn't trust what I saw, because I was willing to believe that my remembered picture was wrong. "Boy, you *were* there."

"But I didn't start any fire!" Briefly Boy's voice becomes gentle. "I was just watching you on the porch, how pretty you looked in the lamplight."

"But if you didn't . . . then did you see my grandmother carry the kerosene can out to the coop?"

Boy shakes his head, but his eyes shift away again. Another lie. He's looking defiant and . . . *afraid.*

"You *did* see Grandmama, didn't you? And saw the first flames, and you let them spread rather than let anybody know you were in our yard, spying on us—"

"No!" Boy says.

Somewhere behind me there's a shout, but I hardly pay attention. All that matters is that I end what I've started.

"Yes!" I tell Boy. "And then, after the fire was roaring, you helped put it out and took thanks for that. Took *thanks* when you might have stopped the whole thing, might have kept Straw Bit from burning! Stopped Grand-mama!"

Suddenly I'm hearing another fire: crackle and pop from the lumberyard. There's more shouting and someone yells, "Don't let it jump to the lumber shed."

"Boy," I whisper. "Not another? Not today?"

I begin pounding on his chest, and with each hit an-other picture snaps into place in my mind; something fits to something else.

"Those other fires—at the depot and the tracks. You *did* set those, didn't you? Just so you could be a hero by helping put them out."

Boy catches my hands, and it makes me more furious. "You're not a hero," I tell him, grasping for words to cause pain. "You're sneaky and vile and ... you're not ever going to live up to your father. Only a coward would try to be a hero the way you did."

Boy's eyes go unfocused with anger, and still I goad him. "Say it, Boy. Say you started those other fires. Or are you *afraid*?"

Boy clutches my shoulders, pushing me against the fence. "I'm not. Take it back, Asia."

"Boy, you're hurting me."

But now Nick is running toward us, yelling, "Let her go," as he shoves sideways into Boy. Boy pushes him back, and Nick grabs him, and then it's Nick holding Boy against the fence.

The two of them glare at each other, and Nick de-mands, "What were you doing to Asia?"

"Nothing." But Boy lowers his gaze, and his words

are almost a mumble. "Telling her nobody calls me a coward."

Nick steps back, looking disgusted. "Maybe you are one, just like your father."

Boy's head snaps as though he got slapped, but now it's Nick who won't stop talking. "Why don't you just tell Asia the truth? Tell her that your father didn't lose his leg saving anybody. He lost it when the trench brace he was hiding behind collapsed. And that he was hiding while his unit went out into no-man's-land without him, without his help. *You know*."

With that, Boy flails out at Nick, and suddenly the two of them are rolling on the ground. Fists jab, hitting dirt and faces and stomachs, and I can't tell who's who but just want it to end.

"Stop!" I say, the word lost between the struggle in front of me and the noise of fire fighting in the lumberyard behind.

They roll again, and Nick cries out as his leg twists under him. And then Boy's on his feet, kicking as Nick struggles up, and I grab the only weapon I see, a short length of two-by-four. I wham it against the back of Boy's legs, sending him sprawling but also catching Nick's arm.

Boy looks up at me, surprised, as if he can't believe it was me who hit him. He half sobs, half whispers, "I'm not afraid."

And then he's on his feet and running away.

Nick holds his wrenched leg with both hands.

Above, the sky is smoky. A man shouts, "I think we got it halted."

27

"WHY DID THE GRISSOMS let Boy tell those lies about his father being a hero?" I ask. I'm home, sitting up late with my parents.

Papa says, "Maybe they were just trying to spare Boy the shame."

"There wasn't any," Mama says. "Lots of soldiers are frightened by war, and this has been a terrible one."

But Papa reaches over to cover her hand. "Not everyone would see it that way, Sophie. And no one could have foreseen how Boy would take things."

"I could," I say, a statement that brings Mama's and Papa's gazes whipping around to me. "If I'd trusted all the pictures I had of Boy, I'd have known he wasn't . . . all right."

For an instant I listen to my words, *wasn't all right.* There's not exactly . . .

And then it's like all the images in my mind joggle sideways one last little bit, nudge themselves into sharp, final focus. *I understand.*

"Boy hated the Germans because the war exposed his father for being a coward instead of the fighter he'd wanted to be. Boy was afraid he'd be like him. He was afraid of being afraid."

"I suppose that could be," Mama says.

"And trying to burn the lumberyard—Mr. Schroeder was just the nearest German."

The war showed Boy his father, and I showed Boy himself. Maybe I shouldn't have done that.

"MAY? I KNOW you're awake, May."

The shoulder of her nightgown is wet from tears.

"May," I ask, "you can't still care for him?"

"I just wish he were different."

"I know."

THE NEXT EVENING Papa calls May and Homer and me into the kitchen to join him and Mama at the table. There are cups of coffee out, an atlas and a calendar, some papers.

Papa picks one up. "You know, your grandmother had a little money left from the sale of her farm. She dictated this to me before . . . a few days ago."

He begins reading, " 'I wish to set aside a sum for my beloved granddaughter Asia, to be used for two purposes. First, I wish a ticket to be purchased for her for a trip to Washington and other northern cities. Second—' "

"Papa," I interrupt. "Is that Grandmama's will?"

He nods. "A short one."

Grandmama goes on to specify that some of her money should be used to help start me to college, or wherever I wish to go after high school, and that like amounts be used for May and Homer.

Her words, almost her voice, seem to echo: "My beloved granddaughter Asia."

"But," I say, and I feel as though my heart is swelling to take up the whole of my body, "I don't want Grandmama's money. I want Grandmama back."

We sit, taking up both more and less space each than we used to, realigning into a family of five rather than six.

BOY DISAPPEARS AFTER the lumberyard fire, leaving just a note that he's sorry about that and about the ones at the depot and by the tracks. He says those are all he set, though, and he's glad they didn't do much damage.

The only way anyone knows where Boy's gone is that a week or so later I get a letter from him postmarked from an army induction center.

"I've joined up," he writes. "Going to try to pay back my debt to everybody."

Boy, boastful and arrogant as always, I think.

But then he goes on, "Asia, I guess I was letting myself believe what I wanted to, and you made me see truth. I guess that's good."

For a moment I measure my two side-by-side pictures of him, Boy open and smiling and Boy hateful. Are they equal, or is maybe the one of him smiling just a little larger?

Which is the truth of Boy? Maybe that answer's not decided yet.

BUT THE BIGGER QUESTION I have is, Isn't it wrong to take something good from Grandmama's dying?

No one gives me much of an answer beyond "Your grandmother wanted you to have this," not until one evening when Mr. Riley's been invited to dinner.

He knows about the proposed trip and the possibility of college and also about my uneasiness in accepting them.

"Asia," Mr. Riley says, "there's going to be some of your grandmother in every picture you ever take because there's a lot of her in you. You won't do her justice if you don't learn to do the best you can."

I can almost hear Grandmama saying, "There's worse people you can take after."

But Mr. Riley's continuing, explaining an idea he's had. "I was thinking, Asia, that perhaps you should assemble some of your photographs to take with you. People at the studios and colleges you visit will be looking for students with talent."

LATE INTO THE NIGHT I turn his words over: *Students with talent.* Is that me? Do I have talent?

"You awake, May?" I whisper.

"Sort of."

"Do you think that even after I've been taking pictures for years and years I'll still be wondering if they're good?"

"Probably. Go to sleep, Asia."

TELEGRAMS GO BETWEEN Papa and Cousin Philip as the details of my trip get worked out.

Meanwhile, I get to see Nick every day. He should be back in classes at A. & M., of course, but his leg needs to heal some before he tries traveling. In that fight with Boy, the tendons and muscles around his knee got torn and pulled every which way.

Also, he's got a huge scabbing bruise on his arm, one that isn't going to disappear anytime soon. "When the fellows at school ask what happened," he tells me, "I'm going to say my girl lit into me with a board."

"You wouldn't!"

"You just wait until the cadet ball. You see if every guy there isn't scared of you."

We're sitting on the porch swing. The evening air is way too cool for us to be out here, but at least we've got some privacy.

We think.

Homer sticks his head out from behind a post. "Hey, Nick," he says, "maybe the army should make *Asia* a soldier. She could scare the Germans into surrendering!"

28

THE ARMISTICE COMES without any help from me.

Fighting stops November 11 at 11:00 A.M.: the eleventh hour of the eleventh day of the eleventh month. Bells ring in Dust Crossing, and the streets are filled with people cheering through a stop-and-start drizzle.

Nick and I sit on a bench holding hands and enjoying the celebration, and he kisses me more than once. "Who's to notice?" he asks when I protest. "Everyone's doing it."

And they are, hugging and kissing and cheering. Some of the people wearing black, they hug and cheer hardest of all. Others, like Mr. Peat, whose son was killed in the last days of fighting, stand silently at windows, watching.

"One more," Nick says, wiping rain from my face and kissing me again.

"Nicholas!" exclaims his mother, and I could die. I didn't know she was near.

"Nell," says Mr. Grissom, "Nick has the right idea," and he gives Mrs. Grissom a huge kiss that sets her blushing and protesting.

Nick holds me tighter, and his ears don't even get red.

IT'S EARLY EVENING before the Grissoms drop Nick and me back at my house. The weather has cleared, and the November dusk hunkers beyond the yellow glow of new street lamps.

"So much is changing," Nick says. "These lights... and I guess now that the war's over, work on the dam will speed up and we'll get city water out here."

"That's what Papa says. He's promised us indoor plumbing. And Mama says that while he's got things torn up, she's going to have more electric wiring put in. She is even going to run a line to the chicken house."

Nick's hand squeezes mine, and I realize we've both been reminded of when the old coop burned.

"It's hard to believe that fire was only eight months ago," I say. "It feels like forever."

"A lot's happened since," Nick says. "Want to go around back to see One-Eye?"

One-Eye is doing fine, sluggish enough to let us know he's feeling winter coming on. I nudge him until he pushes away with scratching feet.

"Not much left of Asia's Zoo," I say. "Just this old fellow and Zoey, and she's become so independent we hardly get to see her."

"Cats are that way," Nick tells me.

But then, like my words were a wish, May answers them. "Hey!" she calls. "We've got a surprise!"

A moment later she and Homer appear carrying a wooden box between them. "Look what we found behind the shed in the lot," May says.

Inside the box is Zoey, along with a huddle of silver-gray and carroty fur.

"They're beautiful," I say. "How many?"

"Five," Homer answers. "May and I are going to take care of them while you're on your trip."

THE MORNING I'M TO LEAVE is cool; crisp air blows up my sleeves and wraps my traveling skirt about my legs. The sky stretches endless miles in all directions, and far, far in the distance a puff of smoke signals the coming train.

Mr. Riley hurries to the platform, a flat, wrapped parcel in his hand. "Asia," he says, "a going away present."

Mama and Papa watch me unwrap a leather folder. "It's a portfolio," Mr. Riley explains, "for you to display your photographs in."

We've been over my pictures time and again, picking my best, printing and reprinting until they are as perfect as I can get them. I think we are both pleased with the results, although Mr. Riley doesn't understand why I won't include my portrait of Grandmama.

"It's your best," he insists.

But in its place I've chosen one I took of my grandmother looking through her old pictures. Centered in it, in clear focus, is the photograph of her when she was my age, wearing her high-collared dress.

Mama nodded when I told her why: "I promised Grandmama. This is the way she wanted to be remembered."

The way she saw herself and the way I saw her, both.

It's as though the very last thing Grandmama has given me is a guide for finding what's true. Maybe I don't quite understand all of it yet, but it's something to live by that's more complicated than "Be proud and keep your backbone straight."

Yes, Grandmama. I hear you. I'll do that, too.

Now Mama is anchoring my hat with a pin and smoothing my coat where it has wrinkled under the strap of my camera case.

"Oh," she says, "see if you can't visit the Smithsonian while you're in Washington, and—"

"Sophie," Papa breaks in, laughing, "if you give Asia any more places to go on this trip, it'll be next year before she comes home."

"But there's so much," Mama protests. "Just think, she might see—"

"Sophie," Papa says, "let Asia see what Asia wants to see. And if you want to go to those museums yourself, then maybe we can save up for a trip of our own."

"Me, too?" Homer asks. "Can I go?"

Off to the side May stands silently, tearful but smiling.

"Wish," I mouth, just forming the word, knowing she'll catch my meaning. In recent days I've said at least a dozen times, "May, I wish you'd come with me," and each time she's shaken her head: No, she doesn't wish it.

Somehow, we've been talking about more than just this trip. Somehow...

Nick, who's catching a later train to school, is in his uniform, leather shoes shining and his shirt starched and stiff. It makes us formal and me shy, until he pulls me aside.

As we walk to the far end of the platform, he says, "Asia, you won't forget me, will you? While you're up north with all those Yankees?" And I can hear that he is only half teasing.

"Probably not," I say, trying to match the joke.

Then I get an idea.

"Nick, let's take our picture, just ourselves. I think we can. You can reach far enough."

I set the Autographic on a baggage cart, propping up the front a bit and cocking the shutter. Nick and I kneel and look into the lens. Laughing, he stretches out his arm.

"Ready?"

This photograph is of Nick and me. It's a bit fuzzy from the camera being too close, but we look as though we belong together. Back to one side, tiny and blurred, are the figures of my family, of Mama and Papa, May and Homer, talking with the Grissoms. Just visible on the other side is the train pulling into the station.